The Saints of God's Country

Edward Craner

Uncle Bob & Betty,

   I hope you enjoy the story!

        EDWARD 9/05

P.S. Long Live the ST. JOE River! ☺

"The Saints of God's Country"
Written by Edward Craner
© Copyright 2005 by Edward Craner
ISBN 1-4196-0911-4
email the author at: <u>edwardcraner@yahoo.com</u>

Order additional copies at: <u>www.booksurge.com</u> or <u>www.amazon.com</u>

First self-published: 1998

Cover art is an original oil painting by the Author's sister, Nancy Beth Myers.

Cover layout by the Author's sister-in-law, Margaret Craner.

Back cover "Elk Bath" photo is a Forest Service picture used by permission – photographed by John McColgan, Alaska Type 1 Management Team, August 6, 2000, in the Bitterroot National Forest, Sula, Montana.

Back cover St. Maries water front photo is taken from a circa 1906 postcard and shows the original St. Maries Hotel and the boardwalk; photographer unknown.

Professional editing services provided by Emily Van Kley.

Foreword . . .

Idaho's St. Joe River valley has been a part of my family's heritage since the 1940's. Both of my grandfathers made their living in the mountains surrounding the logging town of St. Maries, Idaho, which is right in the heart of the valley. George Washington Case, my mother's father, was a forest ranger for the National Forest Service, serving at a post in Avery, Idaho, for many years. Lyle Jasper Craner, my father's father, homesteaded outside of St. Maries in the small town of Benewah, Idaho, and logged in the surrounding mountains. Esther Isabel Case, my mother's mother, raised three children while working as a schoolteacher in a one-room schoolhouse. Hilda Marie Craner, my father's mother, survived the loss of her husband in a logging accident, left to nurture five boys and two girls on her own. This novel was inspired by my family's many memories and the colorful stories about St. Maries and the surrounding area.

The combination of rugged mountain peaks cut by the calm water of the St. Joe and the St. Maries rivers are what make the St. Joe valley God's country. Its beauty is unsurpassed. The town of St. Maries is located where these two rivers converge, and this geographical advantage is what contributed to St. Maries' thriving economy at the turn-of-the-century.

Logs were transported along the St. Joe and St. Maries waterways from the valley's prolific mountains to the developing cities of Spokane, Coeur d' Alene, and beyond.

Although this novel is not meant to be historically accurate, many of the events and characters are taken directly from area history books. If you were to ask any North Idaho native to name the area's most historical event, the forest fire of 1910 is sure to top the list. The fire of 1910 was the worst fire to strike northern Idaho and western Montana in recorded history. Almost three million acres of forest were burned and eighty-five lives were lost battling the blaze, with Avery, Idaho, being the worst hit of the entire area. Millions of dollars were lost by individuals, families, and corporations as timber, homes, equipment, and personal belongings were engulfed by a fire that covered almost 400,000 square miles. Scars from the fire still remain on the mountain slopes and in the lives of the people who lost loved ones, but new growth has replaced the loss, as life carries with it the continuity of change. Time passes and the stories told still echo in the valley where the two saints flow together in the heart of God's country.

Edward Craner, Author, Saints of God's Country

From the Author . . .

This novel is dedicated to my father, Merle Craner, who was raised in the Benewah and played trumpet in the St. Maries High School ensemble, "Mert's Melody Masters," and to the memory of my mother, Barbara Case Craner, who, as a teenager, served sundaes, sodas, and parfaits at Murphy's Corner Store in downtown St. Maries. They instilled in me a love for the area through countless camping and fishing trips up the St. Joe River, Marble Creek, and Homestead Creek. For this, I am eternally grateful.

Special thanks to my wife, Dianna, for the encouragement to make this novel a reality. Your patience, belief in me, and the many hours of editing are what saw this through to completion.

Chapter 1

(North Idaho, Fall, 1979) Weeds grew where the raspberry bushes once were and a mobile home blocked what used to be the fastest sledding run in the Northwest. A few volunteer strawberry plants had survived the summer months in what once was a garden filled with everything that could be grown in the fertile soil of North Idaho. The remains of bird-pecked apples lay nearby, composting in the warm September sun. The surroundings conjured up images of Lenny's youth as he looked down the lot and across the yard toward his grandma's back porch. It had been over twenty-three years since his last visit to St. Maries. There was no particular reason. Family picnics and reunions had brought him to the scenic Idaho logging town as a child and nothing more than the busy pace of life kept him away as an adult.

The back door swung open and Lenny's mom poked her head out. "Lenny, grandma is about ready. Can you bring the car around?" His mom's voice competed with the whistle of a train pulling out of the St. Maries switching yard, which was no more than a quarter mile behind him. He rose to his feet and headed for the house.

"Your grandmother mentioned that a friend of your grandpa's needs some work done on his house. A fence or something. Thought you might be interested," mom said.   "It might help keep your mind off of things."

And help he needed. At thirty-nine, Lenny was freshly divorced and out of work. However, the reality of working alongside some relic who would pummel him with dirges about the 'good 'ol days' was surely less than appealing. But since it was a friend of the family, the expectation was for him to accept. And, the extra money would help take the sting out a lack of steady income.

Lenny backed grandma's mustard colored Dodge Polaris down the narrow driveway and paralleled the front porch.   Mom and grandma lumbered down the stairs leading down from the deck, made their way across the lawn and into the car. "Mom wants to stop by the grave site before we go to the church, Lenny," mom said. He pulled away from his grandma's house, the gravel popping out of the car's tires as they headed toward the cemetery.

"Leonard, you remember where the cemetery is, don't you?" grandma asked. "It's just at the top of the jump-off road from highway 95. Be careful on that blind corner.   Damn County Highway Department needs another death to convince them to do something about that turn.   Lord knows how many letters I've written." She looked around for confirmation from mom and Lenny. "Maybe if one of their own kin gets killed it will wake them up. Lord have mercy on my words."

The truth was that if they fixed the corner, grandma would have to find something else to spend her days worrying about. She had been going on about that issue since Lenny's youth. But everyone needs something to fixate on. Grandma's just happened to be a blind spot on a small side road in a no-name logging town. Lenny took an alternate route to the cemetery.

Mom and grandma checked out the gravesite, added another bouquet of flowers to the multitude, and then got back in the car.

"The services are at the Four Square Church over on Third Street, Leonard," grandma directed. "Get back on the highway toward town. I'll show you from there." He pulled onto the highway and headed for town.

Both of the women seemed to be in rather good spirits considering the circumstances. Grandpa's passing had come suddenly, despite the fact that he had been sick for the past three months.

"Did your mom mention that Jackson Donner is looking for some help?" grandma asked Lenny

"Who? Oh, yeah, she mentioned something about some fence work," he replied.

"Well Jackson's full of vinegar, but he was a good friend of your grandfather's most all of his life.

Besides, he could use your help. If I remember correctly, you used to be pretty good with your hands before you got that desk job."

Mom spoke up: "You remembered right, mom. Lenny was a regular wood smith."

Lenny glanced in the rearview mirror and saw his mom beaming. He had put together two mismatched lamp stands and a rickety bookcase in high school woodshop and she still displayed them in her front room.

Grandma's car pitched from side to side as it rolled to a stop in the church parking lot. Most of the extended family was already there, along with a slew of townsfolk that had come out to pay respects to grandpa. There must have been over 400 people, almost a quarter of the town's population. The church could only seat 150, so most everyone who wasn't family had to try and listen from outside of the sanctuary.

"Remember, Leonard. You're representing the grandchildren. Be on your best behavior," grandma said.

Lenny looked around to see if there was a ten-year-old child sitting next to him. "I'll make sure and keep my back straight and not play with my hands," he said. Mom chuckled in the back seat.

A short, stocky man was coming toward the car. He was about grandma's age, maybe a little younger and wore a faded black suit.

"Go ahead and go into the church," the man said. "The reverend will show you what to do."

Lenny recognized the man from pictures in his grandma's house but was unsure of what relation he was. Seeing his puzzled look, mom explained: "That's Phil, your grandma's youngest brother. He'll be carrying the casket with you. Now hurry on in and take your place. We'll be right behind you."

The sanctuary was packed. The men wore suspenders and boots, and the women wore plain dresses.

Lenny's seat was just a few feet from the wood-hewn casket. A gray haired lady squinted through her sagging bifocals as she sat at the organ, repeatedly playing "The Old Rugged Cross" as people filed by the lifeless body. Lenny stayed seated, bewildered by the thought of looking at a corpse—a piece of clay, sporting a poor make-up job — not something he wanted to remember.

Grandma finally got to her seat and the service began. Friends and family offered the usual niceties, and the reverend gave a eulogy that was on the long side. Lenny's left leg fell asleep about half way into the service and he spent the last half trying to get it to come back to life.

It seemed an eternity until it was time to carry the casket to the hearse. Lenny took his position at the back corner, hoisting the oversized pine box onto his shoulder in sync with five other men. The pallbearers were grandma's brother Phil, her other brother Teddy, Lenny's Uncle Paul, Lenny, and two men who were unfamiliar. Grandma and mom followed close behind as the pallbearers gently placed the casket in the waiting hearse.

So, followed by countless friends and family in their respective station wagons, sedans and pickups, grandpa - Andrew Lloyd Featherweight - was sent on his last adventure, which was the fifteen minute drive to St. Maries' rural Centennial Cemetery.

Headstones and flowers littered the crudely cut grass as they pulled in. People were weeping and the mood was solemn. Lenny looked around and took in the atmosphere. It's not that he didn't miss grandpa - fond memories of childhood trips to the grandparents' house were plentiful. It's just that grandpa was a large, intimidating man who seldom spoke of himself. That's the sorrow that he felt— never knowing who Drew Featherweight really was, other than as a husband, a father and a grandfather. Maybe that was enough. A twinge of sorrow gripped his throat, but it left as quickly as it came.

Grandpa's freshly dug grave stood out, since there hadn't been a burial for some time. The fresh dirt was a welcome contrast to the hard, rocky surface of the surrounding grounds. Lenny took his place at the casket once again. Before bringing it to his shoulders, he noticed the man in front of him, one of the two he didn't know, take a tattered envelope from his pocket and quickly slide it under the lid of the casket. He stood tapping the casket like he was strumming out the last measures of a march of this funeral for a friend. He slowly bent down to the casket and whispered, "There. It's yours now." He looked up, startled that Lenny had witnessed the transaction. He paused for a moment and then looked right through Lenny, as if it didn't matter anymore and wasn't anyone's business anyway. And, it probably wasn't. Still, it sparked Lenny's curiosity. The reverend spoke some more, ladies sobbed and men sniffled; the ceremony ended. Cars drove off as quickly as they came.

People continued to dwindle away until all that remained were mom, grandma, Uncle Paul, Lenny, and the pallbearer that had put the envelope in grandpa's coffin.

"Just how he would have wanted it, don't you think?" mom asked.

"Yep. Except there were too many words said. Drew would have had fewer words." After

Grandma spoke, she looked over at the man sitting next to her, then at me. "Leonard, did you get introduced to Jackson?"

"Not formally," Lenny muttered.

Jackson extended Lenny his hand to shake. He had the grip of a man who knew the value of a hard day's work. "Leonard's the one who's going to help me?" he asked.

"That's right. And don't fill him up with your tall tales of the past, you hear?" grandma said, giving him a whack on the leg.

Grandma stood and slowly circled the grave one last time, then left with mom and Uncle Paul, which left just Jackson and Lenny at the gravesite.

Jackson's folding chair, perched atop discarded rocks and soil, was listing to one side. Jackson and Lenny were both acting squirmish, like a couple of altar boys who'd just been caught red-handed with the sacramental wine. Jackson seemed nervous...or maybe it wasn't nervousness but a cacophony of emotions colliding. Lenny was curious about the envelope and, since he was going to be working beside him for the next few days, finally decided to strike up some conversation.

"Do you need any help getting up?"

"Help getting up? Hell, I'm not going anywhere, son. Your ol' Granddad might have up and left me, but I don't figure on leavin' him for quite some time." He had a smoothness to his voice. Lenny looked down at the ground, not knowing how to respond.

"So, Lenny Dougherty, you're Elle's son."

"Yes sir, I am," Lenny replied.

He motioned Lenny a chair, plucked a piece of cheat-grass from the ground to chew on, and spat at his feet. Here it came - the stories from the "good 'ol days" were about to begin, when men were men and women weren't. Days when . . .

"You're from the city, aren't you?" Jackson asked.

"If you can call Spokane a city," Lenny replied. "More like an overgrown suburb."

"I suppose it's all in what you know," he said. "I grew up northeast of here, out in the Benewah. Any town with a stoplight and two taverns is a city to me."

This confirmed it. Next he was going to tell Lenny that he walked three miles to school, in four feet of snow, using a piece of tarpaper to cover the holes in his shoes.

"Now when I was your age . . . what are you, thirty-five?" he asked.

"Just turned thirty-nine with three kids," Lenny said mechanically.

"What about your wife? Where's she?"

It was inevitable. Elderly people get inquisitive about a man's wife. They're not like the current generation, who quickly make the assumption that a man who shows up without his family is divorced. People Lenny's age are either on their second marriage or wish they were, so they're usually right. He's nothing more than a contributing statistic in the accelerated divorce rate. But people like Jackson were raised in an era where love, commitment and faithfulness meant something. Their values say if you're not including your wife in your conversations, either she's dead or you need a talking to. "We finalized our divorce two weeks ago," Lenny replied.

He looked quickly away and shook his head.

"Were you ever married, Jackson?"

"Yes, son, I was." He stared into the overcast sky. "I lost her to cancer almost two years ago, after sixty-seven years of marriage. She was a beautiful woman; laughed at my jokes and loved me without reservation."

They spoke politely about family for a while before the conversation turned. Lenny found out that Jackson—J.D. as he preferred—went to high school with his grandpa, right there in St. Maries. Jackson chuckled over their fishing trips and other mischief. Hard to believe that Drew Featherweight, the man of few words Lenny had known as his grandfather, was once a kid. It was always easier to think he had been born old.

When the conversation finally started to slow down, Lenny stated, "If Grandpa lived such an exciting life, he surely never let me in on it. He'd never talk about the past. I used to think that something embarrassing happened to him when he was a child, or he was married young and got it annulled, or something . . ."

J.D. paused, took a deep breath, then blurted, "Andrew Jackson Featherweight was a murderer and few people ever knew it."

It was probably the look of astonishment on Lenny's face that made J.D. squirm around in his seat, so much that one of the rocks his chair was propped on popped out, darn near sending him toppling, head first, into Grandpa's open grave. Reaching out, Lenny grabbed him by the suit coat and jerked him back into place.

"Ah, you should've let me go. I'm just going to get us all in trouble if I keep rambling, here." Settling back in his chair, he looked up at Lenny with a four-tooth grin and said, "It's going to be a long afternoon, Lenny Dougherty."

North Idaho in September is as predictable as a mother bear with cubs. While they had been talking, the temperature started to dip, and the sun hid behind looming thunderheads. They were the only ones left in the cemetery except for the caretaker, who was doing a poor job of keeping busy, as he probably thought it would be rude to start shoveling the dirt over the casket while people were still present.   He seemed content, though, sitting under a nearby fir tree. Lenny helped J.D. out of his chair and they walked toward the parked cars. The caretaker acknowledged them with a nod, and then, supported by his shovel, slowly got up from his seat in the grass and headed toward the grave.

"Are you going to tell me more, J.D., or just leave it all up to my imagination?"

J.D. shook his head.   "Me and my big mouth."

They reached J.D.'s truck, a rusted out Ford with rotted side racks, just in time to see the rain fall along with the first shovels of dirt on grandpa's grave. It was as if God had seen fit to water what was just being planted. Lenny attempted to help J.D. into the driver's seat.

"Who in the hell do you think helps me when you're not around?" he quipped.

Lenny got the message and took his place in the passenger's seat.

"Ever eat at Bud's?" he asked.

"Mom used to take us there. Is that grease joint still around?"

J.D. scoffed. "Better than ever. You'll see."

They made their way out of the cemetery, the windshield wipers swiping their way through an erupting deluge of rain.

They pulled up underneath a flashing neon sign that read "_ud's Big Burgers"—the "B" was burnt out. Probably had been that way for years.

Lenny's glasses instantly fogged when the door to Bud's opened. Taking them off, he squinted through the broiled haze, following his newfound friend as he wandered through the tables and slid into a burnt-orange, vinyl-covered booth. He motioned the waitress who meandered over with two cups of steaming hot coffee and then took their order: two slices of raspberry pie. J.D. cradled his cup while Lenny took in the sites of the legendary establishment. Bud's had been around since he was a boy. Grandma always said that there was no way anyone in town could compete with Bud's; they had decent food, the service was usually good, but it was the atmosphere that was unique. On any given evening you'd hear stories of record-breaking logs that had been felled, fish that had been caught, deer that had been shot, with the most recent stories coming from the newly built 9 hole municipal golf course. St. Maries was at the epicenter of tales and legends throughout Idaho, and Bud's was its heart.

It was 1:15 p.m. They had missed the lunch crowd.

"The smells sure bring back memories," Lenny said.

The two made small talk until their order came, avoiding J.D.'s regretful confession about grandpa's past. Finally, J.D. broke in.

"I suppose I owe you the rest of the story," he mumbled, just finishing his first bite of pie. Lenny calmly sipped his coffee and placed the cup back on the saucer, trying not to show his anticipation.

"I'm not sure where to start." He paused to take another bite. "What I'm about to tell you has never been told to another soul and, as long as I'm still alive, can't ever be shared again. Is that clear?"

That seemed a bit much—what was he going to ask for next, a blood pact? Aloud, Lenny agreed, but resolved to reconsider after he'd been told the story.

"You ever hear of anyone talk about the big burn?" he started.

"Wasn't it a forest fire in the early 1900's?" Lenny volunteered.

"A little more than just a forest fire and it was 1910 to be exact, the year your grandpa and I graduated from St. Maries High School with the three others in our class. We were the first class to graduate from the new school building," he said with an air of pride. "It turned out to be a year of hardship as well, and not just because of the fire.

That was the year your grandpa made the decision to become a man—a decision he had to live with the rest of his life."

Lenny settled in with a wary ear to examine every bit Jackson Donner had to tell, as he quickly took them back to 1910 to tell first-hand about grandpa's life.

Chapter 2

(June, 1910) St. Maries in 1910 was a town brimming with hope and promise. Set in a valley surrounded by timbered mountains and intersected by the shadowy St. Joe River, St. Maries was home to loggers, merchants, farmers and prospectors alike. With the first main street in North Idaho to be graveled, even the well-to-do took up residence in its southern hills. It was late spring, and the cool morning air was wet with the smell of evergreens. With just a few weeks left before school was to be let out for the summer, no one was more ready than me and Drew Featherweight. We talked big on the way to the schoolhouse door.

"If there is a God, he must live in St. Maries," I said with assurance. "This is God's country."

"Why would God want to live in this splinter of a town, J.D.??" Drew retorted. "Nothin' good ever came out of here. It's a backward thinkin', redneck livin', Republican votin', bastard of a place."

You had to love Drew, if for nothing else, his crude poetic verse. A man tall and full in stature is often written off as nothing more than a big, dumb brut useful only because he's good on the lift. But not Drew. Studies came hard to him but he had a certain kinship with wisdom, and a depth of character that evaded the rest of us. We all looked to him for leadership, expecting that whatever he did was good. He and I continued to walk along the hard-packed road, rutted from rain two weeks past.

"You figure they'll be logging up on Harrison Ridge this week?" I asked.

"Naw, the oxen wouldn't be able to get any footing on the skid trails. Be more risk than profit." Drew answered. "Besides, logging is a life for men who can't make it at anything else."

That did it. Now I knew that something was bothering Drew. The man grew up in the woods, talked about making his living off of the land, dreamed of raising a family along the banks of the St. Joe River. Why would he talk this way, especially to me, who knew about his dreams? The red-brick schoolhouse came into sight, alive with the sound of children playing. Having kindergarteners through seniors in one building made the school the town's center of activity.

"You still planning to take off as soon as school's out?" I asked.

"Jackson," Drew only called me Jackson when he wanted to make a point. "The day following graduation, I'm going to stand at the city limit and piss me a line across the road. Then, I ain't ever gonna cross it again."

Only a woman could make Drew so sour.

"What about Anna?"

"What about her?" he snapped.

"I figured you'd be waiting on her."

"Well, you figured wrong, J.D."

It was all adding up. Anna was a year behind us in school. Drew and Anna had been seeing each other for the past year-and-a-half. With talk like this, I was confident I'd found the root of the problem.

"You and Anna on the ropes?"

"That's a nice way to put it. It's more like we're out of the ring and cooling off in the locker room."

"It ain't like you to give up so easily, Drew," I said "Why I remember when you got in your mind that you were going to cut down that stand of tamaracks next to your house. You sawed and chopped at those blasted trees for 3 weeks straight. Surely gettin' along with Anna can't be any harder than that?"

Drew stopped at the gate of the school and said, "It'd take less energy to cut down every tree in Benewah County than it would to figure out Anna Schrag."

With that, our conversation ended. We climbed up the stairs to our classroom. Whatever was bugging Drew, he wasn't about to up and share it with anyone. So, I made it my mission to get it out of him, and all I can say is I should've left it alone.

School let out at 1:30, just enough time to hustle the half mile down to the mercantile where I worked stocking shelves and cleaning up. Drew came along; he wasn't due home until dark. We arrived just in time to unload the supply wagon that had arrived from Lewiston.

"Jackson, you and your sidekick there get going on that wagon and I'll send Oliver out to help." It was Mr. Hunt, the owner of the mercantile. He winked, knowing that calling Drew my sidekick would light a fire under him. We turned toward the wagon, with Drew grumbling.

"'Sidekick,' hell, I'll show him a sidekick up his—." Just as Drew was about to explain the anatomical procedure, Mr. Hunts' son, Oliver, jumped off of the loading platform, tackling the two of us from behind. We wrestled each other for a brief moment before Drew had us both pinned in the dirt.

"If you three would use that energy to do something useful, you might make something of yourselves," Mr. Hunt shouted from the back door of the store.

We staggered to our feet, brushed the dust off, gave each other one last jab and went to work unloading the freight.

Oliver Hunt—or Ollie, as we called him— was the third man of our five person Senior Class. The smallest of us three, Ollie was a scrapper, constantly pushing his luck. I think it was because he always felt a need to prove himself. He'd have been in a lot more trouble, a lot more often, if it wasn't for his upbringing. Active in the local church, Mr. & Mrs. Hunt always seemed to do right by Ollie, bringing him up the way everyone wished their parents would—giving rules enough to keep him safe, but at the same time trusting him to be responsible for his own actions. But there was an ornery streak in Ollie, though, which kept him from being the model son his parents hoped for. It's not that Ollie was a bad kid, but his constant questioning of the status-quo often gave people the impression he was a trouble maker. Another factor in Ollie's rebellion was that he and his family were new to town. Though they'd been here since seventh grade, anyone who'd been in St. Maries less than two generations was a newcomer. They'd moved from Nebraska where Mr. Hunt had done well in the brokering of grain. In any case, Ollie always had a chip on his shoulder.

"Hey Ollie, we didn't see you in class today. What gives?"

"Dad-gummit, J.D., why don't you shout it just a little louder so the other side of the country can hear, too!" Ollie barked in a hoarse whisper. "The cut-throats were bitin' on The Joe this morning and I lost track of time. Besides, I'll wager I got more out of whipping that fly on the calm, morning water than you did from your lessons on Galileo."

He had a point there. I must admit that what I learned in school might have helped me to get a job or write a letter, but as far as living was concerned, there wasn't anything like a day with Mother Nature to give you a lesson. There was something about filling your lungs full of fresh air, chewing a splinter of fir, and holding a creel full of trout. Because of his size, you'd never think of Ollie as an avid outdoorsman, but he was the type who'd pack a sack of cracked wheat, a pouch of rolling tobacco, a bed roll and a fly pole and head up one of the nearby drainages into the North Idaho wilderness alone. He'd return two or three days later, smelling like a stray dog, full of stories about his rendezvous with danger, wild animals and the great outdoors. At eighteen Ollie had enough adventure to satisfy a dozen men.

We finished unloading the freight, hurried through the store to gather an armful of snacks, shouted some pleasantries to Mr. and Mrs. Hunt, and then headed for the river. The St. Maries and St. Joe rivers came together in town, making a waterway big enough for commerce and recreation. Because it was spring, sawmills were floating their boom of logs from winter harvest past the town to the mills downriver. The sun was high overhead as we reached the banks of the St. Joe. We dropped to the ground, and choose a well-developed shoot of grass to place between our teeth. Together, we closed our eyes and took in the afternoon rays. Ollie, the self-proclaimed philosopher, said sun on the face could warm a cold heart, weaken the strong and strengthen the weak.

"Where do you get that stuff, Ollie?" Drew asked.

"I don't know, just comes to me, I guess."

"You figure there's anything to it?" Drew continued.

"Sure there is. Don't you feel it?"

"I guess so. I was just wondering if you got it from some book or magazine or something."

Ollie opened his left eye, squinting at Drew. "You have the best seat in the classroom of life where you are. There ain't no school book that can teach you what you're learnin' right now. We always think learnin' is some formal thing you do at the schoolhouse. But it ain't like that." I knew that what Ollie was saying was true, you learn from making mistakes, having success, failing and picking yourself up again. Drew knew it, too, but he had trouble sinking his teeth into it.

"You figure you learn this stuff from God," he asked?

"Maybe. But if you let on to my folks I gave God credit for anything, I'll whip your ass red."

We laughed and we laughed hard, not because it was so funny in and of itself, but because we knew Ollie's bent toward his parents' religion. Even though they hadn't forced it on him, he figured anything they supported, he wouldn't. It was that simple. The truth was his parents couldn't tell him with words what they told him by the way they lived. Even for someone as stubborn as Ollie, a boy couldn't but help let that get to him.

With that, we went on to other subjects, like whether or not the one rainstorm we had would be enough to keep the fire danger down, or what the Rainbow Trout would be biting on this summer. "What do you say we take a trip, soon as school's out?" Ollie asked, eyes wide with excitement. "We'll take my dad's pack horses and go up north of Avery like we've always talked about."

Drew perched his head on his hand and said, "What do you know about that country? Besides, I'm out of here as soon as we graduate. Why would I want to stick around, teaming up with you two—"

"J.D., you still have contact with that family whose son lived up at the lookout?" Ollie said, ignoring him. I couldn't remember the last time Drew didn't jump at the chance to go on a pack trip.

"The Schillings?   Sure, their son is in St. Maries for the month, then heading back up in June to do a four-month term on the lookout east of the Little North Fork. He'd be glad to lend us a hand."

"Then it's settled," Ollie said.

We sketched out some rough plans as to what to take, when to leave, and how long we'd be gone. Drew was hesitant at first, but conceded to stick around until after our trip.

Chapter 3

(North Idaho, Fall, 1979) J.D. paused for a moment from his recollection of the summer of 1910, giving the waitress at Bud's a chance to jump in. "Would you two like to order dinner, or shall I just keep filling those coffee cups?" she asked impatiently.

"Is it 5:30 already?" J.D. and Lenny had been sitting at Bud's for over four hours. They must have drunk a pot of coffee each. Lenny was stunned that he had gotten so engrossed in the story.

"I think we'll wait on dinner, thank you," J.D. quickly said, as he used his index finger to gather up the last remaining pie crumbs.

The two dropped a healthy tip on the table hoping that the waitress wouldn't black-list J.D. for camping out so long. It was a relief to step into the clean mountain air, just in time to see the sun start to drop into the western ranges. The rain had let up, and it looked as if the clouds were going to break overnight. The smell of burgers followed them to their cars. "That's the great thing about Bud's—it's one place that stays around long after you've left!" J.D. said. He thought a moment, then asked, "Why don't we go on over to my house? I'll cook up some elk steaks and show you that fence we're going to mend." Elk steaks—Lenny hadn't had those since grandpa used to cook them in a stew pot over a fire, camping up off Boulder Creek. They got in the truck and headed off to Jackson's.

The old pickup pulled off of Main Street onto a gravel road, entering the part of town the city planners and developers had obviously forgotten. Old cars and motorcycles lined the yards; sagging roofs and drooping porches were a constant of the neighborhood's architecture. Fir trees erupted out of the ground, spiraling up proudly over the other vegetation. A few houses had manicured gardens and yards bordered by fences, but most looked too lived-in for that kind of precise beauty. St. Maries had suffered with the advent of corporate logging, never really able to diversify its economy to compensate. The area that housed Jackson Donner and his neighbors was a departure into the past, a time when a week in the woods would cover living expenses and leave little for extras at the store. Modern progress was almost totally absent from this neighborhood. Missing were the curbed and lit streets; well manicured parks; a neighborhood strip mall, with a dry cleaner, liquor store, video rental and deli; the latest models from Detroit, Japan and Germany; hot tubs, ski boats and R.V.'s; and the people—nowhere near enough to crowd a modern suburb.

Lenny wasn't surprised when they pulled into a weed-choked dirt driveway. He wasn't expecting much, and his expectations were correct. J.D.'s home was perched on a hillside, looking over an acre of property that was more wasteland than beauty. A rotted split-rail fence surrounded it, with gaps of 20-30 feet where it had fallen in on itself. Undoubtedly this was the project that would occupy their time for the next couple of days. The trace of an overgrown garden from the summer still existed, with squash vines starting to turn the same autumn color as the surrounding walnut trees. A compost pile, scattered with coffee grounds, apple cores and spoiled potatoes marked the end of the yard and the beginning of the field. Climbing the rickety stairs to the house Lenny noticed pride and contentment on J.D.'s face as he opened the door. Where did that come from? Granted, Lenny had been laid off, but he had severance pay to cover him until he landed his next job. He lived in a three bedroom, two-bath home on Spokane's South Hill, surrounded by urban sprawl; drove a six month-old car and had a boat in his two-car garage; his membership to the health club could make mortgage payments on his home; and never in his life had he felt prideful and content about walking in his front door. It was a queer encounter.

Stepping over the threshold, Lenny pressed hard on the door until the latch clicked shut. He turned and there, in what he imagined would be a shanty of an interior, were some of the most finely crafted pieces of furniture he'd ever seen.

Not a word of sense came to mind. "The woodworking—it's—beautiful, J.D."

"Just a little something to keep me busy," he said with natural, unrehearsed modesty.

"You made all of this?"

"Yep. I've been working on this room going on ten years," J.D. said. He sighed. "I haven't worked on it since the Mrs. died—guess I lost my motivation."

Lenny took in everything his eyes could manage – a birch coffee table sat in front of a matching claw foot sofa. His and hers rocking chairs sat beside the sofa. Covering one full wall from floor to ceiling was a glassed-in bookcase, full of classics ranging from Twain to Plato, from Thoreau to The Good Book itself. The polished hardwood floors creaked under their feet as they entered the kitchen, which was lined with inlaid cabinetry, butcher-block counters, and a dining set that was on par with those in the Spokane Club at home. Lenny followed the lines of the dining chairs with his fingers, imagining the care that went into each detail

J.D. started preparing dinner as Lenny called his mom at Grandma's house. She'd made up the feather bed in the attic, so he was set for a place to sleep. The two said again how nice the funeral was, and just before hanging up, Lenny heard his Grandma in the background, this time saying not to believe anything an old soot like J.D. Donner had to say, and to watch out for his whiskey: it had a bite worse than a badger. Mom giggled, bid Lenny goodnight, and said that she wouldn't wait up

"How's Anna doing through all of this?" J.D. asked as the phone was hung up.

"Who? Anna?" Lenny gave him a puzzled look.

"Your grandmother. Is she taking Drew's death pretty hard?"

Anna. She'd always been called Grandma Ann.

"She's okay, I guess." Lenny pulled up a nearby stool. "She and Grandpa talked about everything after the last heart attack he had, since the doctor said we almost lost him that time. You're never really ready for it, though." J.D. nodded

After pounding the steaks out, he dropped them onto a hot griddle, greased with lard. The loud sizzle filled the room with a wild smell – Lenny nearly drowned in his own saliva. It was then he realized that, other than the slice of pie, he hadn't eaten since morning.

"It wasn't until I went to Ollie's house one night for dinner that I realized you didn't have to pound all meat to get it tender," J.D. said, grinning.

That was a commentary on his upbringing, not his intelligence. If the only meat your family can afford is so tough it needs to be pounded before it's cooked, then it only stands to reason.

The meal was served: elk steak, red potatoes from the garden, a loaf of sourdough bread baked that morning, and a snifter of sherry. Lenny was curious how his companion would manage the meat with his four teeth, but he seemed to enjoy the process of moving it around from tooth to tooth. They ate until nothing more would go down, pushing away from the table to recline when they were done.

"Did you ever go on the pack trip north of Avery?" Lenny didn't want to keep delaying the story, and he could tell J.D. wanted him to start things out, still unsure if Lenny was being polite to an old man or if he really wanted to be there.

"Yes, we did. But it was the time leading up to the trip that things got complicated. Remember I mentioned that Drew and Anna were having trouble? Well, it was just the next day that we got our first clue as to some of what was going on."

•   •   •   •   •

(June, 1910) I woke with the next morning to the sound of thunder. The dawn was just breaking, but you couldn't tell because of the cloud cover. I remembered Ollie saying that he wanted it to rain to lessen the fire danger, so at first I figured the good Lord had heard his request. Trouble was, I didn't feel a bit of dampness in the air or hear the sound of rain on our tin roof. Jumping out of bed, I pulled on my trousers and bounded down the stairs, meeting my father at the front door.

"Is it dry lightning?" It was a question I didn't have to ask. The look on his face spoke for him.

"Yeah, that it is." He went upstairs, out his bedroom window and climbed to the peak of the roof, the highest place on our property. From there, father could see over our twenty acres and the surrounding hills and mountains from which he made his living. My father was a logger, complete with a bull team and a five-man crew, and a fire this time of year meant certain destruction to little operations like ours. I knew he'd keep watch until the storm had passed. Knowing there was no chance I'd get back to sleep, I elected to get an early start on my chores. Since it was Saturday, I'd have the rest of the day to pack and plan for our getaway to Avery. Drew and Ollie depended on me to get things organized, saying I had the mind for it. I suppose it was their way of being lazy; but it didn't bother me – I enjoyed putting things in order.

The storm broke by mid-morning. It had only caused a brushfire north of town where a bolt of lightning hit an old tack shed. Neighbors had it out in a matter of hours. Scares like those left the people jumpy for the next few days, and rightly so. Everyone depended on the woods for their livelihood, even if you weren't a sawyer, skidder or choker. The town dentist had started in the woods himself, and was said to spend his vacation days pulling green chain at the mill just to keep in touch with his past. Yes, everyone was a logger in St. Maries. The only difference was whether you wore suspenders and cork boots, or supplied some service for those who did.

I met Drew and Ollie at the mercantile just before noon, all of us hoping that Ollie's mom would take pity on our sweaty faces and feed us lunch. It usually worked—today was no exception.

"I got some hot roast beef just out of the oven. You three lugs willing to eat it?" Mrs. Hunt gave each of us a look as we entered the back door that led through the mercantile and into their attached home. She knew we weren't getting away with anything; it was clear she got as much satisfaction out of serving us as we did from eating. The table was set with metal plates and glasses, a checkered and tattered tablecloth, and mismatched silverware. We all knew the Hunts had enough money to outfit themselves with silver and fine china, but it wasn't like them to spend money on things that didn't do something useful. Mrs. Hunt hollered through the door for Mr. Hunt, who was just finishing with some customers. He hurried to the head of the table, taking his place for the prayer. My eyes met with Drew's, who glanced over at Ollie. Each of us was thinking that this was what we had to suffer in order to get a free meal. My sympathy went out to Ollie who had to sit through this three times a day.

"Bow your heads, Jackson, Oliver, Andrew. And close your eyes," Mr. Hunt said gently. We did both quickly, since the one time Drew thought he'd be funny and only close his eyes, he got a firm smack on the back of his head from Mrs. Hunt just after the prayer had begun.

"Dear Lord," he always started that way. "We thank you for the food we're about to eat, the day you've provided for us, and the life you've given us to live. Bless these boys and their ways." Here it came, the clincher that made us each cringe in our seat: "As you look down upon every action they take and every thought they have, we ask they be in line with your plan, not theirs. Amen."

I swear every time Mr. Hunt did this, he looked up afterwards with a smirk. Once again he'd reminded us that our actions were always being watched, if not by he and Mrs. Hunt, then by the all-seeing eyes of the Almighty Himself. Luckily, the food and company were well worth the agony of that moment.

"So, you fellas heading up The Joe to Avery, eh?" Mr. Hunt said around a mouthful of roast and carrots.

"That's the plan," I said.

"That's a mighty long way, well over a week on foot."

We looked down at our plates, knowing that the one who spoke first would be the target. Drew's appetite got the best of him.

"Could you pass me the gravy, please?"

"Sure, Andrew," Mrs. Hunt said.

"Drew, can you be gone from the homestead for that length of time?" Mr. Hunt was enjoying his game.

Drew nervously ladled the gravy over his entire plate of food. "We were thinkin'," he paused to lick his fork, covered in gravy at the bottom of his plate. "We were thinkin' maybe we could borrow a couple—of—" He looked our way for support, but got nothing.   "You see, Mr. Hunt, we were wondering—" By this time, our friend who was giant in stature was like a five year-old asking for a licorice stick from the candy counter. Finally he forced it out, "Would it be alright if we took three of your pack horses? If not, I'm sure we could have just as good a time hiking up to the fast water of The Joe and setting camp up there."

"Now why in the name of all that's sacred would I want to give my quarter horses to three hide-binders like you?"

Drew paused to chew and swallow. "Uh . . . I guess you probably wouldn't."

Mr. Hunt sat back in his chair, a smirk returning to his lips. Just then the bell rang on the front door of the store, signaling that customers had come in. He pushed away from the table and left the three of us still twitching with nervousness. Mrs. Hunt, knowing well what was happening, carried on the mealtime chatter. "Andrew, are you still courting Batum Schrag's daughter?"

"Yes ma'am." He paused for a moment, then said, "Well, sort of."

"What's that supposed to mean?"

Drew fidgeted with his food. "I'm not sure she's that interested in seeing me anymore. Every time I ask to call on her, she gives me some two-bit excuse. At school she's still awful friendly. I believe she has me a little confused."

Mrs. Hunt forced a smile, and then quickly let it fade. "Drew, it has nothing to do with you. Anna is a sweet girl, and you're plumb fortunate to have her as your friend." Since I'd known the Hunts,

I never knew Mrs. Hunt to gossip or say one bad thing about another person. That's why what she said next struck me so hard. "The truth is, I'll bet she's afraid to let you see her at home. Not only is that good-for-nothing father of hers trying to ruin his life, but he's ruining his children's, too." Mrs. Hunts' face was red. "You stick with that girl, Andrew. Don't let a little confusion get the best of you."

Mr. Hunt came in from the store. Mrs. Hunt smiled. "Can I warm up your plate, honey?"

"No. I'll take it into the store and eat behind the counter. Too many people wandering in and out." He gathered his plate and utensils and walked back to the door. Just as he was heading over the threshold, he looked over his shoulder and said, "Ollie, best be making sure the two geldings and the gray mare have good shoes on them before your trip." Grins appeared across our faces.

After finishing our meal, we thanked Mrs. Hunt and made our way to the door. As we went out, Mrs. Hunt grabbed Drew by the arm and whispered something in his ear. He listened intently, nodding his head. She gave him a hug, and then bid us all goodbye. "Don't forget that the shelves need to be stocked and the floors swept after supper, Ollie," she said. We let the screen door slam shut behind us, fully knowing we were one step closer to our dream of a pack trip to Avery. I looked over at Drew. By the look on his face something was weighing heavy on him.

"You guys go ahead and I'll catch up in a while," Drew said.

"Where you headed?" Ollie asked.   Drew hesitated. "Listen Drew, if something's bugging you and you don't want to talk about it, that's okay. But if you're thinking that you can run around all alone and make things better, then I'm here to tell you that you're a darn fool." Ollie's straight-shooting cut to the quick, especially with Drew. "If you're going to do something stupid, at least let us enjoy it, too!" Ollie said.

We all laughed, and then Drew got serious. "I gotta go see Anna," he said.

Chapter 4

Avery was nothing more than a wide spot on the soon-to-be Union Railroad. It was some fifty-five miles up the St. Joe River from St. Maries, and had originally been established as nothing more than a lookout base for the Forest Rangers and fire watchers. It was accessible about six months out of the year, while the other six months it was blocked off by snow. The intrigue we had wasn't with the railroad or the fire watchers, though, it was with the wilderness, the untamed beauty of the area surrounding Avery. While, we didn't actually have to go more than thirty minutes to find solitude and the untamed wilderness, the idea of blazing our way into uncharted territories (uncharted for us, anyhow) gave us a charge. There were logging roads, Forest Service roads and trails leading up there, and those were going to lead us to our Holy Land, the area that we decided was the ultimate place for being, just being—not one of us was sure what we meant by that, but we were so confident regardless. For now, though, plans for our journey were put on hold for a more pressing issue, that of Anna Schrag.

We wandered along Main Street just long enough to realize a small obstacle to our pursuit: "Do either of you fellas know where Anna lives?" Drew asked.

Ollie looked over at him in disbelief, "You've been courtin' this gal for over a year, and you don't know where she even lives? Blasted Drew, what if she would've said 'yes' to you callin' on her—what'd ya done then? Ask her for a map?"

"I'm 'bout certain she lives out toward Cherry Creek, but ain't exactly sure where."

"Let's stop off at Handy's for directions," I said before Ollie could continue. "I know Old Man Schrag stops in there to get his cross-cut sharpened at least once a week. Maybe he'll point us in the right direction." Handy was the local blacksmith. His real name was Andy; he got his nickname because he had but one hand. He lost his left hand about eight years earlier when a huge stock wagon stopped in to have a weak wheel looked at. Trying to save time, he blocked it up with the horses still hitched, and just as he got the wheel pulled, one of the team spooked, pulling the wagon off of the block and toppling Handy over. The exposed wheel hub caught his arm just right, severing the hand at the wrist. Folks said that he picked himself up, went into his shop and seared the open wound closed with a poker that was sitting in the hot coals, then went back and finished the job. All we knew is that it seemed Handy had been around forever and he always welcomed us when we happened by. As we approached his shop, we could hear his swearing and carrying-on over the blaze of the blacksmith's furnace.

"Shiiii . . . if I get one mo' of these basta's in here, I'm gonna have their nougats."

We turned into his shop just in time to see him finish shoeing a mule, holding up its leg by wedging it between his stub and his own leg, while his good hand hammered like the dickens.

"Having some trouble there, Handy?" Ollie asked with all of the forthrightness of a paying customer.

"Boys, this is where they comed up with the sayin', 'stubborn as a mule.'" Handy gave a couple more whacks to the shoe, then let go of the hoof and gave the mule a jab in the ribs with his elbow, a last shot to remind the beast who was boss. "What can I do fo' you, no-goods?" he said with a grin through his soot-covered face. It was strange: Handy was somewhat educated, but his language patterns were particularly lazy, especially with slang. He had directed his question at Ollie, whom he knew best because of the mercantile.

"We were wonderin' if you knew where Ol' Man Schrag lived. We were goin' to pay him a visit." Handy hesitated, lifted his hat from his brow and wiped the sweat from his forehead with his stub, leaving a black streak of soot and grease.

"Now, why in the hail would you three rasca's go out botherin' that ol' basta? He's just shy of a hermit, an' sure the hail don't want any comp'ny from you." He reached down and picked up a pair of tongs that he had made special for his work, having widened the handle of one side just big enough to slip his stub into. "Why, he catches you on his prop'ty, he'll taken 'em little nougats of youse and squish 'em!" With that, he motioned to us with his tongs.

Drew and I winced, but Ollie just kept on going. "Actually Handy, we were headed out toward Cherry Creek for a delivery from the mercantile, and Drew here wanted to see if Anna was at home." Ollie was smooth with such stories.

"Why the hail dint' ya tell me 'twas for romance? That makes all the dif'rence in the world. Me bein' a sufferin' romantic me-self, I s'pose I'm partial to young Mr. Featherweight's plight." He grabbed for the other hoof of the mule. "When ya git to the Cherry Creek bridge, go south at the next dirt road—his is the homestead 'bout a half mile on your right. Cain't miss it – he's got 'bout ev'ry kind of wreck around his place, ev'rything from old wagons to busted up steam donkeys. Like I said, cain't miss it."

We thanked him and as we headed down main street toward Cherry Creek, we could hear Handy, "Dad-burnit, mule, I'll make dinner outcha if you don't — you basta! This be the last pissin' on me you'll ever do."

Joking about Handy and the mule got our minds off our mission. When the Cherry Creek bridge came in sight, we stopped. We hadn't spoken about what we were about to do, let alone why. "What is it that's got you so determined?" I asked Drew.

"J.D," he paused to think it through, "you ever known Anna to wear any make-up?" Now this was an angle I hadn't anticipated.

"What in sam-hell does that have to do with—"

"Just answer me, J.D. Does she wear any make-up?"

I pictured Anna in my mind, her fine features that didn't need a layer of disguise, and then quickly concluded, "No, I reckon I've never seen her with anything covering up her skin."

"Me neither," said Drew. "What business, then, would Batum have buyin' make-up, if it weren't for Anna?"

Ollie piped in, "Suppose he's got a sweetie— a bit of make-up would be a right-nice gift, wouldn't you think?" Drew and I looked over at Ollie, wondering where he got that notion. Batum Schrag was the antithesis of a gentleman, keeping his distance from almost everyone, especially women.

Chapter 5

We stayed until the sun started to dip behind the hills. The silence hadn't broken for the better part of an hour, and the boy had stopped whimpering and gone in, so we decided the immediate danger was over. We made our way back through Batum's rubble piles, and headed back toward the bridge that spanned Cherry Creek. The water was running but just a trickle. Years like this, when the snow pack was all but melted because of an early spring and the rains were slow to come, it was a hard go for little tributaries like Cherry Creek. Other times water was plentiful and it bubbled with trout, pushing the limits of its banks, feeding nearby Lake Chatcolet along with dozens of other small streams.

We stopped at the bridge before we entered onto the main road. The water drifted slowly, mocking our solemn mood. Then, the cool evening hurried us along, our shoulders tight and hands plunged deep in our pockets. Ollie hummed as we walked, a poor rendition of "Red River Valley." We walked into town and split at the mercantile agreeing to meet the next morning on the boardwalk behind the St. Maries Hotel after Ollie got out of church. Ollie disappeared into the warm light spilling out of the plate-glass front window. Drew and I watched Mrs. Hunt give Ollie a welcoming embrace, then playfully whack him on the butt with the broom he was to use to sweep the store. I'm confident we were both pondering the contrast with what we had just seen. How could it be that someone as ornery and ungrateful as Ollie had two parents to love, support and encourage him while only a few miles away, a young woman and her brothers lived in fear every moment their father was home, or in dreadful anticipation of when he'd arrive. The real frustration came not just in knowing about the injustice, but in the reality that there wasn't anything significant we could do to change it. Drew and I turned from the window and walked the rest of the way home in silence.

•   •   •   •   •

The St. Joe was flowing at its usual slow pace, and though the water level was two feet below normal, it felt like Sunday morning business as usual. The boardwalk behind the St. Maries Hotel, where I was to meet Drew and Ollie, gave front-step service to the steamers and travelers fortunate enough to afford a night there. The hotel was the most elegant spot for miles, with its rooms and dining area overlooking the water. The boardwalk ran along its back side for a number of blocks, bordered by businesses and boats. This morning, two river boats were tied up along the dock, and people were shuffling on and off. These were grand vessels, churning water from stern paddle wheels as they moved up and down the river connecting St. Joe City to the east and Coeur d' Alene to the west. The boats were the heart of commerce for the St. Maries and St. Joe valleys; the largest of the fleet, the Georgie Oaks, was over 150 feet long and 25 feet wide. It could carry up to 200 passengers with all of the luxuries, including a restaurant, bar and staterooms for first class passengers. On lazy summer afternoons, we would sit and watch people of all sizes, shapes and styles make their way around the docks. Inevitably, there would be a fight, or a small catastrophe of some kind. Whether it was a family out for an afternoon cruise on the river or a few 'dandies' in their Sunday best trying to catch the eye of a young lady, it was cheap and consistent entertainment. I spotted Drew with his feet swinging over the edge of the boardwalk and his eyes closed, taking in the sun. I sat down next to him.

"Can't see the sights like that, Drew."

Keeping his eyes shut and swinging his legs in a constant rhythm, he said, "I'm tryin' to learn, you know, like Ollie said."

"Any luck?"

"Did you know the Georgie Oaks' engine hum is higher than the Spokane's? And when a mosquito flies past you, it sounds thinner than a fly?"

I guessed his head was full of smoke from the steamer.

"Drew, what the hell are you talkin' about?"

"I told you, I'm learnin' like Ollie does." He opened his eyes, squinting in the flood of sunshine. "Did you know people who get on the river boat barely speak, but you can't keep the people quiet when they're gettin' off? And the smells: bacon cooking at the hotel, wet cedar floating past, women's perfume staying around long after they're gone—what a combination!"

"How long you been out in this here sun, Drew?" I asked.

A shrill whistle interrupted us—it was Ollie, coming at his normal pace, more like a trot than anything. You'd think even Ollie'd move slower on a Sunday, but to him, if it was worth getting somewhere, it was worth getting there fast. Didn't seem to matter what day of the week it was. Ollie was dressed in his Sunday britches, loosening his necktie and unbuttoning his collar as he walked. He sat down on the other side of Drew, who'd closed his eyes for more instruction from God.

"Can't see the sights like that, Drew," Ollie said.

"He's learnin', Ollie, just like you showed him," I replied. "He figured out the Georgie Oaks sounds different than the Spokane, something about mosquitoes and flies, and he smells a lot, too."

"Hell yeah, he smells. Probably hasn't had a bath in days!" We got a chuckle out of that, but Drew kept his face focused. After Ollie and I milked the joke for all it was worth, Ollie asked, "What's God saying now, Drew?"

Drew cocked his head back, keeping his eyes shut. "Shhh. He's speaking right now, telling me to get up and—" He stood up, grabbed Ollie and hoisted him over his head, threatening to hurl him into the water.

"Now Drew," Ollie shouted, his voice crackling and panicked, "I just got done talking to the Good Lord myself, and he didn't say anything about throwing me in the river! Maybe that was just your stomach growlin'." How Ollie ever got out of predicaments like that, by ridiculing Drew, I never knew. The folks on the boardwalk gave us a wide berth, probably thinking kids like us should be out working the fields instead of causing trouble around town. We were lucky, though, to come from families that knew not only the value of a hard day's work, but that of a healthy dose of leisure, when appropriate. My parents had homesteaded in 1887, when St. Maries was nothing but a few buildings at the confluence of the two rivers. When I was born in '93, my dad and older brother had already cleared thirty acres of timber, selling it to the mill at Harrison, about 10 miles downriver toward Coeur d' Alene. The returns gave them enough money to start a small logging operation, contracting with the federal government to log regulated land. Even when times were hard (and they usually were), dad made it a point to be home for supper with the family. Once we finished our chores, our time was our own; I always felt I got a fair shake from my folks. And although both Drew's parents died of the croup in '01, he, his brother and two sisters were lucky to be raised by his Aunt Maye and Uncle Herb, who couldn't have children of their own I say we were lucky because we had the privilege of being young while we still were.

The mid-day sun was straight overhead and beating down when Drew finally let Ollie down. Leaning on the rail waiting for something to happen proved unprofitable. I was about to suggest a swim when Ollie broke the silence. "Let's go see if we can get a glimpse of Boathouse Nellie," he said. Drew and I jumped up, interested at the proposition.

Nellie was a whore who lived on a crude houseboat at the east end of the boardwalk. Nellie wasn't just any whore, she was the sweetheart of the town, the jewel of the river, the one who kept the loggers trapped in sin on Saturday nights and the preachers busy prying them out on Sundays. Nellie was such a celebrity, in fact, that the mayor gave her a key to the city, saying she was responsible for the decrease in gun fights and brawls since so many men had started visiting. The town paper, the St. Maries Gazette, once even featured Nellie as "Person of the Month." The following week though, they withdrew the honors without explanation. Rumor had it the editor's wife had threatened to withhold from her husband the very thing Nellie made profitable if he kept up with such 'whore adoration.' The closest Drew and Ollie and I came to Nellie's charms were Sunday afternoons, when she'd drape her undergarments around the boat to dry. It was enough for us to fill in the fabric with our imaginations.

We wove our way in and out of the people crowding the docks toward Nellie's boathouse on a custom made landing that kept the waves from disturbing other boats docked nearby. We stepped from the boardwalk to the riverbank, and continued up a side street to Main until we came to the access road for Nellie's launch. We paused, as we did every time we came to this point, wondering who would be first down the well-worn trail. Drew and I both looked at Ollie.

"Do you two realize," Ollie said, shifting his eyes toward the river, "how pitiful you look when you don't have the guts to make a move?" With that, he thrust past the bordering bushes and down the trail. Drew and I fell in behind. I'm not sure why we were nervous—we'd never had any trouble. I guess thinking what would happen if we were caught by anyone we knew. Not to mention, the mere fact that we knew what went on within on those few square feet of water was enough to make a rugged man shake. Ollie slowed as the trail opened onto the river. Four-foot walls had been built on the approach so that certain men could crawl from the privacy of the brush onto the boat without being identified. We side-stepped the approach and jumped down onto the silty shore of the river so we could get a better view of Nellie's laundry hanging to dry.

"Something ain't right," Ollie whispered as we bunched together. "There ain't a stitch of clothing anywhere." Where there was usually a colorful array of lingerie we saw only the faded wooden boards of her deck. A spiral of smoke came from the stack of her living quarters, which was strange considering the warm spring day.

"Maybe she's sending her laundry out to be washed," I said.

"Yeah, or maybe she isn't back from church," Ollie joked.

"Maybe you should listen to Jackson more often and wag that tongue of yours a little less, Oliver Hunt. Maybe you'd learn something for once." We jerked our heads around and there, standing at the head of the approach, was Phoebe Stockman, the fourth member of the Class of 1910.

Phoebe was no ordinary girl. Though she was raised in a town that weathered men and women long before their years, Phoebe had skin the color of fine china, hair the color of night, and facial features delicate and fragile as a porcelain doll. It didn't hurt that her parents owned the only bank in town—having every luxury surely played a part. But with Phoebe, style and class were inherent to her personality. Her mere presence often stilled a room, not because of her beauty (which was nothing to scoff at), but because she had the confidence and forthrightness of a woman twice her age. Phoebe Irene Stockman was the peach of St. Maries: voice of the weak, advocate of the downtrodden, and friend for the lonely. Just then, though, she seemed the goddess of our demise.

"Phoebe, fancy seein' you here," Ollie scrambled. "Drew and Jackson were intent on seeing if Miss Nellie needed any groceries from the mercantile, and seein' as it's Sunday and all, I figured a good deed was in line." Drew dropped his eyes so fast you could almost hear them hit the ground. I got a sheepish look on my face and stared off into the afternoon sky. But Ollie stood there and grinned, obviously banking on his charm and wit.

"I think the only deed you figured on doing today was filling your eyes with as much of Miss Nellie's undergarments as you could. And if that's what you came for, here's your fill!" Phoebe took a wet pair of bloomers from the basket she was carrying and flung them at Ollie, nearly knocking him over with the weight of water-soaked material. You see, Nellie was no petite thing. In fact, she outweighed most of her customers, so even the smallest of her undergarments consisted of a few yards of material. Drew and I jumped away from Ollie, fearing we'd get something worse, like a brassiere or a corset. But Phoebe knew Ollie was the instigator and therefore only saw fit to punish him.

Ollie peeled the bloomers from his face, which had become red with embarrassment and dripping with water. "Something tells me you question our motive, Phoebe."

Contending with Ollie, Phoebe held her own. "You, Oliver Hunt, have a keen sense of the obvious. Not only do I not believe you, I think you're a bunch of perverted voyeurs. Furthermore, if you don't hustle your guilty little hinnies up that trail and unload the rest of Miss Nellie's laundry for me, I'll make darn sure your antics reach the proper channels." We obeyed—hustled back up the trail, snickering as we went, partly out of embarrassment, but also excitement as we were not only going to see

Miss Nellie's undies, but carry them as well. That was more adventure than we'd reckoned for. We each grabbed a basket from the back of Phoebe's wagon, and then returned to the dock.

"Do you do this for Miss Nellie every week?" Drew asked, trying to be natural and unassuming.

"When Miss Nellie came in to make her weekly deposit at the bank, I could see she wasn't feeling well. I guessed it wouldn't be good for her to be out washing clothes in the cold water," replied Phoebe, who was busy arranging and sorting. "So, after the preacher's sermon about helping widows and orphans, I decided to see what I could do for Miss Nellie." She paused, then qualified, "I don't have to love the sin to love the sinner."

Much to her parents' chagrin, Phoebe lived out her faith in day-to-day activities. I imagined her keeping company with a whore would send them into a tirade, about her safety, priorities and reputation. It's not that her folks were bad people— they were regular attendees to the local community church, gave generously to charities and fund raisers, and were even known to give unsecured speculative loans to loggers based on the next year's yield (although the interest rates were often criminal). But, as much as they wanted to instill a strong moral character in Phoebe, they cringed when she acted out her faith. It was only the winter before that she'd gotten it in her head to make the community centers and churches into temporary hostels. She figured since they were used only occasionally during the week, all the men who didn't have a warm place to sleep could put a bedroll on the floor or one of the padded pews. It was her interpretation of loving your neighbor as yourself. It was hard on her, as she quickly came to understand that for most well-meaning people, the adage translated to "Love your neighbors when it's convenient, economical and logical. Otherwise, let them fend for themselves." After being shunned by every organization but her own church, she was more determined so she converted the loft of her family's hay barn. There were linen-covered straw ticks for sleeping, an oil drum stove, and a whiskey barrel with its top cut off, filled daily with fresh water for drinking and washing. On any given night there were between five and ten men who called the loft their home, with an occasional woman gracing the premises (who Phoebe would invariably bring in to the main house and sleep with her in her own room—she said a barn didn't offer the creature comforts that were befitting a lady). In short, Phoebe Stockman lived what she believed regardless of her parents' concerns about her security or tarnishing their good name.

Phoebe finished sorting the baskets, handed each of us one, and motioned us onto the launch to

Nellie's boathouse. Here, things got tricky. We had never set foot on the launch, let alone been confronted with the possibility of crossing it. It's not that we hadn't fantasized about being there, but we'd certainly never pictured ourselves accompanied by Phoebe Stockman. She was a vision of purity that drastically contrasted with the happenings of the boathouse—like driven, mountain snow splattered with axle grease. Reality took the wind out of our preconceived, fantastical ideas about this trip. We were about to meet Boathouse Nellie the human being, not the mythical play-toy for men.

Drew, Ollie, and I warily followed Phoebe. Each creak and groan of the wood underneath our feet startled us, confident that the town folks could hear it from their place at the supper tables. I was tempted to crouch below the four-foot sides of the launch. When I looked over my shoulder, both Drew and Ollie were bent at the knees and hunched over, waddling along with the grace of a catfish tossed on a hot rock. Evidently I wasn't the only one with visions of anonymity.

We made it to the deck and waited as Phoebe knocked on the door, which was constructed of rough-cut 1x10's and a sign that read, "If you choose to wear your caulked boots inside, there won't be nothin' to do but whip your hide; if that suits your fancy just fine, then why the hell come here and waste my time!" Ollie, Drew and I looked down at each other's feet, and then suddenly remembered that none of us had a pair of caulks.

I heard a bed squeak inside, which sent a rush of blood through me, making me feel as if my temperature had just topped out at 105 degrees. I clutched my basket and readied myself to meet Boathouse Nellie face-to-face. Visions of her raced through my mind, all incomplete since the closest I'd ever come to her was the brush that lined the river bank, a good forty or fifty feet away. Footsteps approached, Phoebe identified herself, and the door swung open. There, draped in an ankle-length cotton nightgown, was the legendary "Whore of the Valley," Boathouse Nellie.

Chapter 6

(North Idaho, Fall, 1979)   The grease from the elk steaks had hardened in the pan, ready to be left overnight in preparation for morning eggs.   Two hours had passed since J.D. and Lenny pushed back from the table. The sherry had run out and the cool night had set in. Lenny had so enjoyed his time that he hadn't noticed the discomfort of the beautiful but very hard chairs.   He was surprised when J.D. suggested a jaunt outside to see his woodshop. Lenny's bones creaked and muscles groaned as he lifted from his seat.

They stepped out into the bright night. The cloud cover had lost out to the stars and moon – you could almost touch the Big Dipper and with a bat long enough, reach out and give the moon a whack, speeding its orbit around the earth.   There was something about being up in the mountains and away from it all—maybe Lenny was starting to understand why the three boys thought their trip to Avery so important.

The two shuffled along a dirt path to the detached garage. Just as he noticed there was no doorknob, J.D. lifted with his toe a small, hinged board that appeared to be part of the entryway. This revealed a miniature cavern that ran underneath the door to the inside of the shop; inside the cavern was a wooden lever J.D. stepped on. The lever lifted the latch on the other side of the door, letting it swing inward, an ingenious invention.

"Either I forget the blasted combination to the padlocks or lose the keys," J.D. said, embarrassed. He reached into the darkness and pulled a cord that lit up a couple of naked bulbs in the center of the room, revealing a modest, well-organized, and well-used shop, complete with a pot belly stove in the far corner; a lathe, table saw and radial arm saw in the center; a drill press opposite the stove; and a rack of boards lining the near wall. Small bins and shelving were interspersed, holding such necessities as nails, screws and hand-tools.

"Let's get a fire going to take the edge off— this here Franklin will have it warmer than a sow's back in mid-July." J.D. placed a little wad of paper on the grate, covered it with some meticulously split cedar kindling, and then struck a match on the side of the stove. In no time the fire was ablaze. They toured the shop, J.D. giving a history of each item. He had hand tools his father had made when he was a boy, power tools that hadn't been updated since he'd bought them decades ago, and a ceiling hung with failed experiments. After they had made their round, J.D. stopped off again to feed the fire, which already had made a noticeable difference in the room's temperature. Taking down some ears of corn that he had drying over the stove, he asked if Lenny had ever had parched corn. J.D. didn't wait for an answer, but grabbed a cast iron skillet from the side of the stove, blew out the sawdust, dirt, and cobwebs, and set it on the stove top. From a nearby shelf he took a small tin, popped the top and dipped his fingers in, pulling out a mound of what appeared to be bacon grease. He swirled it around the pan as it heated.

"People eat hominy, popcorn and those corn nut snacks all the time, but never figure out that it all comes from the same thing." J.D.'s common sense was beginning to seem like ingenuity, or at least charm.

The smell of bacon began to fill the room. J.D. pulled the dried kernels from the cob, gently scattering them across the skillet. They sizzled, reviving the appetite that two hours earlier they swore would never return. J.D. sprinkled a dash of salt over the kernels, then let them cook, turning them a few times until they were golden brown. Using a paint scraper he'd wiped off with a dirty cloth, he scooped the cooked kernels onto a newspaper he'd laid over the shop bench. He snatched a handful, tossing them back and forth in his hands until they were somewhat cool, and threw some in his mouth. Once again Lenny marveled at his chewing ability—it made him think of how Handy must have looked trying to shoe that mule with only one good hand. He tried the crunchy, slightly puffed kernels and thoroughly enjoyed them.

"It was on the way to Avery I first tried parched corn," J.D. started. "Drew's uncle loaded us up with a slab of cured ham and dried corn, since Ollie's folks had agreed to provide the horses."

"So all you did was drop off the laundry after you met Nellie?" Lenny asked. J.D. chewed another handful of corn.

"Hell, no! I guess I need to fill you in on the rest of that afternoon."

•   •   •   •   •

(June, 1910) Nellie asked Phoebe who the three ghosts were who were carrying her laundry—I guess we looked as nervous as we were. Phoebe giggled and told us to put the baskets on the back side of the deck so she could hang the damp clothes out in the afternoon sun. We all offered to help Phoebe so that we didn't have to face Nellie alone.

"You boys get your tails in here out of the sun. Phoebe's an able soul. She can hang the laundry on her own," Nellie said. Ollie and Drew decided to play coy, so I was left to lead us into Miss Nellie's quarters. I took a deep breath, and walked right across the deck. My bravery surprised us all; Drew and Ollie didn't take a step until I was through the door. My heart set speed records in my chest. Once inside, it was warm and stuffy, partly because of the glaring afternoon sun, and partly because of the pan of boiling water on the stove probably to help clear Nellie's ailment. Drew and Ollie finally made it past the threshold.

"You boys could probably use something cold to drink, couldn't you?" Nellie offered through a raspy cough. We hesitated, then nodded together. Even smooth-talking Ollie was short on comment, a state I don't recall being repeated.

"Take a seat and make yourselves comfortable," Nellie said. "I'll just be a minute getting this lemonade ready."

I looked around, assessing the seating options. Ollie and Drew were right in front of a parlor couch that had barely enough room for the two of them, leaving Ollie to hang off of the end. I continued to scan the room, starting to panic. In Nellie's line of work sitting wasn't a priority. I was considering dropping onto the wooden floor when Nellie confirmed my fear: "Pull up a seat on the bed, young man—chairs aren't plentiful in these quarters." She winked.

The bed standing in the corner was adorned with a flannel spread and embroidered lace pillows, a queer contrast to its barren metal frame and tarnished brass headboard. 'It's no big deal,' I told myself as I took a step toward the bed, but I couldn't help thinking what took place there, countless times each weekend. I suppose it was silly, but at the time it was as if the bed was a creature in and of itself. I imagined the relationship it had had with Nellie's clients and being lumped with those faceless customers was terrifying.

Nellie seemed to read my mind. "Don't worry," she said. "You'll be sitting there as my guest, not my customer." I had been discovered, my fear and timidity exposed. "In fact," she continued, "wish I had more handsome gentlemen visitors who sat on that bed expecting nothing more than a glass of lemonade and a bit of conversation." She broke a smile. "So, I promise not to tell anyone you shared my bed if you'll have a seat next to me." My heart slowed, joints loosened, and breathing returned to normal. We all grinned. I made my way over to sit next to Nellie, who had handed Drew and Ollie their glasses and was holding mine in her outstretched hand from her position on the bed.

We chatted until our lemonades emptied, signaling it was time to go. Reluctantly, we made our way to the door where Nellie was standing. "Phoebe, thank you so much for your kindness—I'll be fine taking the laundry down. You're a sweetheart for thinking of me."

"You make sure and do that before the sun sets and the temperature drops," Phoebe replied."

"I just want to leave them up long enough to let these boys get a good look—hell, that river bank must be fifty feet away, a strain even on eyes as young as theirs." Phoebe laughed and we blushed with guilt. Nellie hugged us and kissed each of our cheeks as we left.

No one said a word on the way back up the trail. Usually we returned from a boathouse adventure whispering about what we had seen or wished we had seen. But that day we were working toward adulthood, having learned that behind every mask and title is nothing more than an honest-to-God person. Phoebe thanked us for our help and we said good-bye, and then headed back to do some preliminary planning for the Avery trip before our Sunday afternoon had slipped totally away. The sun was making its way toward the horizon and since we each had to be home by supper, we stopped at the mercantile to put the trip together on the Hunts' kitchen table. It was a productive evening. Mrs. Hunt allowed us enough ginger cookies to kill our adolescent hunger without spoiling supper. Mr. Hunt wandered in from the store where he'd been rearranging shelves. He sat down with us and grabbed a handful of cookies.

"Where are you at in your plans?" he asked.

"The way we figure, it'll take the better part of four days to get there," Ollie started. "And that's if we catch the riverboat to the mill just west of St. Joe City," Drew added.

"They'll let you on with the horses?" Mr. Hunt asked.

It was my turn. "The Georgie Oaks and the Spokane won't, but there's a supply barge that makes weekly trips and we can work for the fare by helping with freight."

"Do they know what a bunch of slackers you are? They'd be lucky if they get one man's labor out of the three of you!" It didn't take much to figure out where Ollie got his tongue. Mr. Hunt shook his little frame as he laughed, joined by his wife who couldn't resist. Undaunted, we continued to list supplies, routes and safety precautions.

Chapter 7

A morning haze had set in. The cool air condensed on the surrounding ferns, spruce and bear grass. Low clouds hung in a scattered pattern, hiding the peaks of the surrounding mountains. Their absence muted the grandeur of the range. Still, the smell and sight of the evergreens, their cool damp penetrated my bones. It seemed impossible then that drought was an ever-present threat. All of us were hard-pressed to imagine that the collage of colors and shapes that made up the North Idaho forests were in danger of becoming fuel for a raging wildfire. But all the same, it was true. We'd seen it before and, as my father so often reminded me, we'd "for damn sure see it again." It was just a matter of when and to what extent.

I snatched one of my mother's biscuits from the kitchen table on my way to do the morning chores. The buttermilk taste warmed my mouth as I fumbled on my boots like I did every morning, my tired mind having a difficult time keeping up with my active body. Lacing my boots proved especially hard with the bread hanging from my mouth, my eyes half-open, and the light from the breaking day inadequate to see detail. It was rare that I'd show up at breakfast with all of my eyelets laced, my shirt matching my trousers, or my hair anything short of a bird's nest.

The spring on the screen door was tight. It slammed behind me. The bull team stirred, knowing a fresh load of hay was coming and the chickens started their squabbling-the feed from the day before was pecked over. Then there were the two plow horses. Since they had a whole pasture to graze on, their dependency on me was limited. Each morning they would stand on top of a small rise, silhouetted against the morning sky, looking down as if the rest of us were their kingdom. This would last halfway into the feeding, when they would see the rest of livestock getting all the attention. Not wanting to miss out, they would nonchalantly meander down the slope to the fence, where I'd greet them with a carrot or cube of sugar and a scratch behind the ears.

I worked through my chores, finishing with my favorite of all the animals, the pigs. I think it was their masked intelligence that intrigued me. Their reputation does them no justice, portrayed as dirty and lazy animals worthwhile only for Sunday ham or a morning side dish. There was a time I didn't know any better either, until one afternoon when I spit out a piece of gum in the middle of the pen while I mended a length of fence. I went in the house for a drink and when I got back I noticed that the gum was gone. Figuring the pigs had covered it over or it had simply sunk into the muck and mire of their stall, I didn't think anything of it. When I brought their slop the next morning, though, I noticed the boar chewing intently. Knowing that they usually finished their feed the night before, I was puzzled. Reasoning that it could be the last of a snake he'd caught, I continued, pouring the rancid bucket that made up their breakfast. The boar went over to the corner of the pen, spit out what he was chewing on and made his way to his trough. There in the corner was the gum I'd discarded the day before! I watched, amazed, as the boar completed his meal, then quickly returned to the pen's corner where he picked up the gum and once again started chewing it. From that time on, those who visited our place began spitting their gum into the pig pen for the boar, who was joined quickly by the sow. The ritual became so popular that my dad finally made a sign and nailed it to the pen's gate. It read,

> *Spit if you must your wad of gum,*
> *The pigs are happy for more,*
> *The sow prefers the sweet fruit kind,*
> *With spearmint favored by the boar.*

We had to add a line later asking folk to refrain from spitting their chewing tobacco into the pen because a slug of chaw made the pigs dizzy, so their stumbling and frequent falls proved hazardous to the piglets underfoot.

Following breakfast, my father and brother loaded up the wagon, hitched the bull-team, and made their way off to camp where they'd meet the rest of dad's crew for a week of logging in the woods. I never told my dad, but those were tough times, watching he and my brother leave me behind to tend to the domestic chores. I longed to be present when the old-growth cedars and firs came crashing to the forest floor. Some of the trees were so large it took a week for two men to fell and cut them into lengths manageable enough to skid to the nearest flu. The summer before I had spent two weeks up on Mica Creek where my brother and father were cutting. Since the creek wasn't high enough to float logs down, we built a splash dam. When we had a good bunch of logs ready, we sent two scouts downstream, making sure there weren't any other operations in the area. One stayed at the mouth of the creek and the other returned to report that the coast was clear. Then, we placed charges of dynamite throughout the dam. Igniting them blew the dam and sent a rush of water and logs tumbling down the creek, into the waiting St. Joe River. The scout at the mouth had to pay attention, since the sound of the dynamite was the only signal he had to head for high ground and avoid being caught up in the mass of timber, rock and water. Such displays of power left me longing to play a part in the action that came along with life in the woods. Certainly I had romanticized the job, disregarding the frigid winters and blistering heat of late summer. Still the lure of the woods had me, just like it kept each generation of loggers going back year after year, despite the uncertainty of success or failure, returns or losses, and frequently, death. The summer of my graduation I was anticipating the woods near Avery without any thought of harvest or profit. I met up with Drew at the main road, as I did most mornings on my way to school.

"Still feel like pissing a line at the city limit?" I asked.

"Naw, that was a knee-jerk reaction to Anna. I suppose you figured that out, though."

Drew was sporting a fresh-washed shirt with a starched collar. His boots had been polished, and his hair slicked with enough grease to make a hundred wagons run smoothly. He didn't make eye contact, probably hoping if he didn't look at me I wouldn't notice he was all dolled up. When a breeze picked up and blew a waft of cologne I had to speak up.

"Shoot, Drew, you smell good enough to eat!"

"Dad-gummit, J.D., I knew you couldn't keep to yourself." His complexion flushed red as he fixed a matted lock of hair that had fallen in his face from the weight of the grease. "If you're spouting off, Ollie will be ten times worse. I'm liable to sock him as soon as he opens his mouth." Both Drew and I knew he'd never hit Ollie Still, I decided I would warn Ollie once we arrived at the school. A little prevention might save our trip, not to mention a friendship.

I tried to relieve Drew's embarrassment "Anna's going to be right proud to see you, Drew." I should have left it at that, but couldn't resist. "And if she ain't, I'm sure the stench from that cologne will beckon girls all the way from Coeur d' Alene!" Luckily he laughed. We continued on, with Drew more talkative than usual, due, probably, to his newly found favor with Anna. The encounter the weekend before seemed to have sealed Drew's commitment to Anna, which, in turn, had given Drew hope for life after graduation.

We continued along the well-known route to the school yard. As we approached the gate, I found it hard to believe that in less than two weeks, we were to be released into a world that didn't know we were coming nor cared, for that matter.

The halls echoed as we stepped through the doorway, the new tile floors barely scuffed. The whole building wasn't even a year old, a far cry from our old schoolhouse, which had been a makeshift operation in the city's community center. Our classroom looked as it had all year, with a map of the world on an easel in the corner; a chalkboard covering the front wall of the classroom, thick with leftover chalk from months of lessons; Miss Sorensen's pine desk; five rows of four lift-top desks; a stool in the corner opposite the map (to which Ollie often found his way after a comment the teacher deemed inappropriate); a row of windows that opened onto the adjoining play field; and bookshelves that housed many of the works of contemporary historians, poets, scientists, and journalists on subjects ranging from dry-land farming to the plight of the Black American.

Tenth through twelfth grades were all in the same classroom, with the other grades spread throughout the rest of the building. This meant that at any given moment Miss Sorensen would be pummeled with questions about first-year algebra, directly followed by how "augur" was to be properly used in a sentence, and then by whether it was "One if by land, two if by sea" or the other way around. To teach high school in St. Maries you had to be well-versed in subjects at several different levels—you had to know your way around philosophy, mythology and history, had to teach and write the English language well, and interpret a wide range of sciences—all of which Miss Sorensen did. Why anyone with her credentials would want to hole up in a mountain town like St. Maries baffled me. Miss

Sorensen said living in St. Maries was a gift because she had been raised, like Ollie, in Great Plains of the Midwest. She'd come out with her cousin's family who homesteaded out towards Benewah. She regularly reminded us that North Idaho was heaven on earth and informed us that if we had any sense at all, we'd appreciate it.

Even though Miss Sorensen was attractive, she intimidated her gentleman callers with her intellect and knowledge of worldly matters such as politics, fashion, religion and commerce. We referred to these types of men as 4-44's, which stood for a 44 inch chest and a size 4 hat: big and dumb. I should say that she intimidated every man except our own Oliver Hunt. His confidence was undaunted by the fact that she had a college education, was almost ten years his senior, and had no interest in him. He actually believed she had taken a liking to him, and it was his belief that he had more to offer than the other men of the area, what with his charm, self-proclaimed intellect, and promising, if undefined, future. His persistent references to her beauty and charm earned him the frequent trips to the corner stool.

Drew and Anna sat at the back of the classroom talking back and forth most of the day. Drew's hair stayed in place. In fact, the sheen of the grease illuminated Anna's dark complexion, giving a glow to their corner. One could only assume that all was going well. Ollie had shown great restraint as a friend and a man interested in self-preservation, by not commenting on any of it.

"Class," Miss Sorensen said, "before you are dismissed, I would like you each to write a one page essay on what you'll be doing in twenty-five years." Two weeks earlier, Miss Sorensen had asked us to start thinking about our futures and what we wanted them to look like. She said that it was a great help to her when she was young to write down what she wanted in life, something about visualizing your dreams. "Remember, it doesn't have to be exhaustive, but should contain information on your proposed vocation, where you'll be living, family statistics such as a spouse and children, and any physical facts you feel would be pertinent." She hesitated, then said, "Any vows or promises you'd like to include are encouraged. I won't be reading them. Instead, I'll seal each envelope and send them to you in 1935. You have my word." If there was one person we could trust, it was Miss Sorensen.

Drew leaned over towards me and whispered, "Are you going to shoot straight or play it safe?"

"I don't think she'll open them, if that's what you mean," I replied. "Anyway, chances are, the only thing honesty will get me is a good laugh when

I'm old enough to need one!" I chuckled, but Drew's stony expression told me his was giving it a lot more thought than I was. He took a quick look over at Anna, furrowed his brow and started writing.

Ollie was first to be finished. Turning in his essay, he whispered loudly, "You're free to read my essay, Miss Sorensen...especially since you're in it." She ignored him and the rest of us did, too. Still, he was awful proud of himself and strutted toward the door like a bridegroom. He gave a wink, signaling for us to hurry so we could make the most of the afternoon. As he turned his head back he smacked square into the closed classroom door, making a racket that echoed down the hall. His ego was bruised, but he made a wise crack and continued on his way out the door, humming a tune.

The rest of the class finished. Students folded their essays and placed them on Miss Sorensen's desk. She would carefully put each one into an envelope with the student's name already on it. Some students would hang on to their work, making her snatch the papers from their grasp; some would quickly drop them in front of her and dart out the door; while others boldly handed their essays to her, acting as they'd just written the Declaration of Independence. I dreamt up a whimsical situation in which I was the captain of a riverboat and had married a stewardess. Together we delivered customers up and down the St. Joe River. We owned the boat and our children were the crew. Greeting and entertaining, they were known throughout the valley as the "Singing Donners."

I finished my essay and gave it to Miss Sorensen. Drew and two other tenth grade boys were the only ones who hadn't finished when I left. Generally speaking, Drew struggled with writing, so I guessed it might take a while for him to finish. I found Ollie sprawled underneath a willow tree outside, nursing his newly injured nose.

"Those classroom doors aren't much on the give, are they Ollie?" I said.

"No sir, but you can bet Miss Sorensen will remember me whenever she gives that assignment."

"Did you really write something about her in your essay?"

"I most certainly did. You know, it's those little things that make a teacher's day, when a student makes a fuss over her, especially when they have charm like mine."

"Oliver Hunt, you couldn't charm a snake, let alone a grown woman!"

We jerked our heads around to see who'd been listening and found ourselves in the company of Phoebe Stockman and our other female classmate, Isabel Wainwright. It was Isabel who had spoken.

"You're just jealous because it wasn't you who I wrote about," he said.

"Yeah, watching your prince walk into a closed door would melt any woman's heart." Isabel, like Phoebe, enjoyed putting Ollie in his place, a task that needed doing on a regular basis.

Isabel and Phoebe were quite a team. Everything Phoebe was, Isabel wasn't, and vice versa. In contrast to Phoebe's fine features, Isabel had a square jaw, broad shoulders and protruding cheek bones, all capped with curly, dishwater blonde hair. She dressed in men's clothes, threw a ball like one of the guys, and could tie a fly with the agility of a seasoned veteran. You wouldn't see Isabel drinking tea on Saturday afternoon in the dining room of the St. Maries Hotel; instead she'd be hanging out at the docks finding out what the fish were biting on. All the same, she and Phoebe were bound together. There were times Phoebe would try to get Isabel to wear a dress and a ribbon in her hair, and on occasion Isabel would invite Phoebe over to work in her garden. They'd even occasionally indulge each other. For the most part, though, they honored each other's differences like good friends do.

Ollie promised to buy us all sodas at Miller's Corner Drug Store if the girls agreed to wait with us for Drew. We passed the time reciting what we had written in our essays until Drew finally stepped through the schoolhouse doors. He still had that serious scowl and was walking stiffly.

"So, Andrew, who's your princess going to be?" Phoebe asked.

Drew grimaced, "I don't put any stock in those essays—even if I could figure out what I'd be doing in twenty-five years I wouldn't want to."

"I enjoyed dreaming about my future, Andrew, and so should you."

Drew couldn't cuff Phoebe like he would Ollie for a statement like that. He just had to stand there and take it.

"Ollie, let's go get that soda. You still buying?" I asked, trying to save the moment. We stood, brushed ourselves off and headed down the road toward Miller's Corner.

Chapter 8

Like any destination in St. Maries, the trek to Miller's Corner wasn't far. Ollie took the lead, not because anyone asked him to, but because it was his nature. I swear, if Ollie had had a twin, they would have raced for the birth canal. We would invariably let him walk ahead and his leadership would often take us on alternate routes, up side streets and through fields that had special points of interest ranging from a flowering bud on a perennial, to the carcass of a dead cat. Yes sir, it was always an adventure following the footsteps of Oliver Hunt. On this particular day, though, the dusty roads and hot sun took some of the pleasure out of the journey. Even though June hadn't yet arrived, summer was well underway, evidenced by the turning of the field grass. St. Maries usually received enough rain to keep the underbrush green, until midsummer, when it would begin to brown. This year the fields were already tan from the lack of rainfall. This complicated more than the scenery; it made the surrounding roads and trails billow with dust from any movement by foot or wagon. Summers with such harsh conditions were unusual for the St. Joe Valley. Even the mountains, with their usual abundance of vegetation, were struggling to keep food available for deer and elk. Many of them were forced to make their way out of the high-country to seek food. Weakened, malnourished, and exposed, they were easy prey for the mountain lions that followed them down from the hills. These cats were commonly seen by loggers and rangers, but it was only during drought conditions that town folk would make their acquaintance. Phoebe and Isabel had had a chance encounter one hot summer's day a few years back, though few of us knew of it and those who did were sworn to secrecy lest Isabel pound our heads in.

Late one August afternoon, Phoebe and Isabel were attending a picnic with Phoebe's church group. Phoebe had pleaded all week for Isabel to go with her and when she gave in Phoebe agreed that she 'owed' her friend for making such a sacrifice. The picnic was held on the St. Joe, just east of St. Maries in a meadow that banked the river. It was ideal for swimming and sunning since it was well into the slow water that led into St. Maries. The day was blistering hot, and they cursed themselves for forgetting their bathing outfits. After an afternoon of three-legged races, picnicking, softball, and horseshoes–of which Isabel was declared champion—the two ladies considered stripping to their bloomers and submerging themselves in the deep green waters of the St. Joe. I think Isabel would have gone through with it had it not been for Phoebe; the thought of being thrown out of the congregation for indecent behavior at the church picnic did not sit well with her, and she was confident that her parents would take the same view.

Phoebe and Isabel were the first to leave that afternoon, coaxed largely by Isabel's complaints about the heat. The two of them mounted the horse they had rode in on together, and headed back toward town. Isabel kept up her complaining so that after about ten minutes, Phoebe turned the horse off of the trail toward the river, then gave him a kick and rode the two of them right into the water. Isabel didn't have time to do anything but laugh. Along with the horse, they cooled down in the crisp waters of the St. Joe.

After a time, they were confronted with the fact that they would have to ride the rest of the way in soggy clothing. Phoebe decided there was no way she wanted to be seen in such disarray, so they decided to disrobe and let their clothing dry on some nearby rocks. The surrounding trees shielded them from the trail, and as long as they were quiet, no one would know they were there, dressed in nothing but the outfit that God himself had given them. And it would have worked had it not been for a hungry mountain lion who was taking interest from the riverbank on the other side. In a matter of seconds the horse caught sight of the lion, spooked like it was a whole pack, and tore loose from the branch to which he was tied. Isabel and Phoebe jumped up from the rocks, trying to grab the reins and calm the horse. The horse would not be calmed. He climbed up the river bank onto the trail and headed toward town. Phoebe and Isabel grabbed their clothes and leapt onto the trail, managing only to pull their blouses over their heads as they pursued the fleeing horse. As soon as they realized where they were and what they were not wearing, they panicked and turned around to take cover in the bordering brush again. Their timing was perfect. They spun around just in time to see the church goers, led by the good Reverend himself, come around a bend in the trail. I'm sure the two must have wished it was the mountain lion! Flustered they turned again and made a run for their horse.

They say that the land speed of a human is governed by two elements: ability and terrain. That day an additional element was added: absolute terror. Phoebe and Isabel made it to their horse and raced down the trail until they felt safe to dismount and finish dressing. Back in town, they decided to behave as if nothing had happened, hoping the church-folk might have thought that what they saw was nothing more than a pair of spooked white tailed deer. They knew it was a stretch, but the alternative was just too humiliating. And, much to their pleasure and surprise, nothing was said—until the following Sunday. As Phoebe sat in the second pew with her parents on either side of her, as she did each week, Reverend Turlick decided to deviate from his six month series on the book of Revelation and address a more "relevant and pressing" issue, taken from a text in Proverbs 7.

> *"And behold, a woman comes to meet*
> *him, dressed as a harlot and cunning*
> *of heart. Her feet do not remain at*
> *home, she lurks by every corner and*
> *around every bend in the trail."*

At this point, Phoebe felt the eyes of the entire congregation piercing the back of her head like darts thrown in a bar room. Pinned between her parents, she dabbed her forehead with her hanky, despite the cool breeze making its way through the room. Reverend Turlick continued:

> *"With her many persuasions she*
> *entices him, with her flattering lips*
> *she seduces him. Suddenly he*
> *follows her, as an ox goes to the*
> *slaughter."*

"It is the lamb in the lion's clothing that you must guard against," he said. "Worse yet, the innocent-looking temptress with little clothing!" That's when Phoebe fainted. Blacked out, right in the middle of Reverend Turlick's sermon. The best part of the story is that Reverend Turlick had been talking about old man Franklin's latest jaunt to Boathouse Nellie's—not about Phoebe and Isabel. It turned out that the Reverend was near sighted and wasn't wearing his glasses at the picnic. He'd seen nothing more than the horse being chased by a couple of white-flanked Indians. He'd shouted back at the picnickers to freeze where they were until the danger passed. Phoebe blamed her fainting on the heat and the story ended there.

•   •   •   •   •

"Hi, Mr. Miller," Isabel said, barging through the screen door. "Hope you have enough ice cream to serve this bunch of sorry-sots." Miller's Corner was the only ice-cream shop in St. Maries and Isabel spent most of her afternoons working there.

Mr. Miller greeted each one of us with a wide grin. Miller's Corner was your typical soda shop—it had a bar you could belly-up to if you wanted to watch the concoctions being made; stools with spinning tops that were fun until you'd spun one too many rotations and felt like your ice cream was going to erupt out of your stomach; and authentic ice cream chairs with matching, glass-topped tables. Mr. Miller had them imported all the way from Sweden, where he'd grown up working in his parents' ice cream parlor. With the fuss he made over them, you'd think they were cast in gold instead of the wrought iron that made up their frames. Granted, it was beautifully ornate ironwork, but to sit in one comfortably for any length of time was impossible. To Isabel, Mr. Miller had admitted that was precisely why he liked them so much—more comfortable chairs might entice people to linger beyond the time it took to finish a soda or malt. Isabel took down our orders on a napkin, and then handed it to Mr. Miller, who had lined up five fountain glasses, all ready to receive a massive helping of ice cream. Isabel rolled up her sleeves and took up the scoop.

"Bel, you put that away—you're the customer today, not the help."

"Aw c'mon, Mr. Miller . . ."

"Don't you go arguing with me, young lady."

With that, Isabel set the scoop back down and took her place next to Phoebe at the counter. Mr. Miller went to work, dishing and scooping the flavors with the skill of a master. He knew exactly how much ice cream each glass could hold, poured the soda with large hand gestures to add drama, and finally, like a last brush stroke, he placed cherries atop each of his masterpieces.

"So, ol' St. Maries is finally getting rid of you bunch of hooligans," he said, pushing the heaping glasses toward us.

"Not for another two weeks, yet."

"Twelve days, Phoebe, not two weeks," Ollie quickly corrected.

"A little anxious, are we?" asked Mr. Miller.

"With all due respect, I don't know if 'anxious' is a strong enough word." Ollie took a long drink. "See, me and J.D. and Drew are all headed up to Avery on a pack trip the day after graduation and aren't figurin' on returning until we're darn ready."

Mr. Miller finished wiping the counter and set the serving utensils to soak in a container of water. "Now what do you boys know about that country?"

"What's there to know? We just follow the St. Joe drainage 'til we hit the ranger station at Avery."

Mr. Miller leaned over the counter. "What about crossing the river when you hit the canyons above Calder? Do you know where the eddies in the river are? They'll swallow you like a fly with the water this low. And what, in the name of all that's sacred, are you going to eat during this trip? Your family's mercantile doesn't have a delivery service that runs that far east now, does it?"

Ollie took another gulp and then paused to wipe the corners of his mouth. "Details, Mr. Miller, nothing but details," he said.

I looked at Drew, who was looking at Ollie, undoubtedly thinking the same thing: pretty damned important details! Ollie and Mr. Miller went on to discuss the terrain. Mr. Miller had logged near Avery with two of his cousins, also first generation Swedes. They talked about routes and landmarks, challenges and obstacles. All the while Phoebe and Isabel were holding their own conversation on the other end of the bar.

"Are the young ladies accompanying you gentlemen on your journey?" Mr. Miller asked.

Ollie leaned over the counter and whispered loudly, "We said we wanted adventure, Mr. Miller, not frustration and headache!"

Mr. Miller leaned in, too, and whispered back, "Do they intimidate you little man?"

Ollie recoiled, bracing his arms across his chest. To Drew and me Ollie blurted, "The day I'm intimidated by a female, I want you two to take me up on Harrison Ridge and shoot me."

Mr. Miller laughed.

"What makes you think we'd want to go along even if we were invited?" Phoebe said. "Who would want to hang around three wanna-be men, days removed from soap? They'll have to survive on fish, since their stench will give them away to any other game." Mr. Miller grinned again, recognizing Phoebe as winner of the war of words.

He turned back to us. "You know, there's Little Lost Lake south of Avery. You ought to include that in your travels. It's worth the trip itself. My brothers and I used to meet there whenever we'd be off on separate jobs - -. I'd give you directions, but I'm sad to say that I can't remember all the landmarks." He topped off our glasses with another scoop of ice cream. "You know who could tell you, though, is Jacob Schilling. He's in town to pick up some supplies, then heading back for a term on a look-out east of the Little North Fork of the Clearwater."

"What's so special about this lake, Mr. Miller?" Drew asked.

Before answering, Mr. Miller placed his utensils back to soak and meticulously wiped the counter with a cloth he'd draped over his shoulder. He worked his mustache with his hands and peered out the window as if he saw the lake just outside. "Andrew, have you ever had a religious experience?"

Drew looked puzzled, and then answered, "When I was five and my mom and dad were still alive, I remember having a dream about heaven. Is that what you mean?"

"What was it like?"

"Well—" he paused. "It was peaceful—without distraction. It made me never want to leave. "

"I couldn't have said it better myself," Mr. Miller said. "The water at Little Lost Lake is clear, like a deep cut of glass without any flaws. From the time the sun peers over the eastern range to when it dips into the west, there's no such thing as time. It's beautiful, nothing short of beautiful." Mr. Miller turned away. "I buried my youngest brother up there, under the tallest Tamarack tree I could find. He developed pneumonia one fall when we were logging, got too weak to travel. I reckon if I ever get the chance to get back, I won't leave." Mr. Miller drew a heavy breath, clenched his teeth, and said, "That's what is so special about Little Lost Lake, Andrew."

"Sounds like a place where God would live, huh?"

Mr. Miller was startled. "Yes, Andrew, that's exactly where God would live."

Chapter 9

Ollie charged the sodas to his parents' account. Mr. Miller reminded him he'd have to make up the difference if his parents refused. We each pledged our word as witnesses and made our way out the door. After an unhealthy amount of Mr. Miller's ice cream, we groaned with each step jolting our glutted stomachs on the stairway down. Whoever said you could never get too much of a good thing had never had a double-scoop soda at Miller's Corner.

The two ladies went their way and the three of us went ours, across the street to the mercantile. Ollie and I had freight to unload and as usual, Drew came along to pass the time. Mr. Hunt was on the loading dock having a discussion with the wagon driver when we arrived.

"I ordered a dozen sacks of flour. You bring me a dozen sacks of cracked wheat and ask me to be flexible and adapt. Well, I'll just ask my customers to 'be flexible and adapt' when they complain that their pancakes are as fluffy as shoe leather and their bread is as light as a lead ingot!" Mr. Hunt was getting his point across loud and clear.

"Look, it's an honest mistake, Franklin. To make it right with you, I'll take back any you don't sell when I make deliveries next week," the driver replied.

"Darn straight you'll take it back." Mr. Hunt was cooling down when he saw he wasn't going to be stuck with the surplus. "Double the flour order on your next delivery, Stu, and I'll see if we can get by with what we've got. If not, I'll put these hawn-yawks to work crushing the cracked wheat with a sledge and anvil." He nodded our direction and hoped there wouldn't be a big rush on flour next week.

"J.D, you and Drew unload Stu's wagon while we finish the paperwork. When you're finished, hitch the team and take our delivery wagon down to the docks to pick up the freight that came in on the Georgie Oaks from Coeur d' Alene. Mrs. Adamson's Wurlitzer finally arrived. She'll meet you down there at 3:30. You come with me, Oliver. Your mother needs your help placing the goods." Ollie scowled. 'Placing the goods' was a term for rearranging everything in the store so it would look more appealing to customers. In short it was decorating, something Ollie loathed.

"Aw, can't I go to the docks with J.D. and Drew? They might need my help with the Wurlitzer."

Mr. Hunt stopped what he was doing with Stu. "This is not up for discussion, Oliver. Do as you're told, please," he said.

It ended there. Ollie kept his scowl, but made his way up the stairs, across the loading dock and through the store's back door. Before he and Stu disappeared through the door, Mr. Hunt said, "Refresh Mrs. Adamson's memory of the terms of our agreement if she contests the delivery charge. She always tries to get out of it. If it gets ugly, which it can with the Adamsons, show her the signed invoice. It's under the seat in the leather satchel." Drew and I moaned about our overloaded stomachs, and then threw ourselves into the freight, unloading the sacks of cracked wheat, cans of vegetables, bolts of cloth, and crates of everything from 30-30 shells to Wenatchee-grown apples.

After hitching the team, we made our way onto Main Street toward the shipping docks on the other side of the St. Maries Hotel. The long, narrow road passed the passenger docks and opened onto a small area where wagons jockeyed for position to load and unload their goods. It was the commerce district of the valley, where merchants from all along the river came to exchange their wares, hoping for a better price, lengthier terms, and bigger orders. Although it was relatively safe, there had been a scuffle or two within the last few months. In one a dock worker was killed in a knife fight when an out-of-town trader accused him of skimming goods. The trader had nearly been beaten to death by the rest of the dock crew when the sheriff showed up.

We spotted Mrs. Adamson right away, which wasn't surprising. With the girth of an old-growth cedar and a bonnet with a feather curling out of it, in a sea of men dressed in overalls and dungarees, she was easy to spot.

"Yoo-hoo, boys, right this way." Mrs. Adamson made us the immediate center of attention. I drove the horses toward the dock, then circled around and began positioning the wagon for loading.

"You're backing up crooked, young man. Pull forward and try again."

Backing a wagon was never my forté, so her advice was less than welcome. Nonetheless she was the customer, so I endured.

"Yes ma'am, Mrs. Adamson," I said. After moving forward, I pulled back on the reins again and the horses responded well.

"That's it . . . keep coming . . . and stop!" Mrs. Adamson came up to the buckboard and continued directing. "Get on down here and help me check this container out. I ordered this all the way from Seattle. It'd be a wonder if anything made that kind of a journey without some damage, especially the way these commoners handle the freight." Being that she and her husband owned the St. Maries Gazette, Mrs. Adamson could say darn near anything that came to mind, a privilege she exercised regularly. We obliged her request, prying back the boards so she could see that everything was intact.

"Yes, yes, very nice. All of the keys seem to be in place and none of the pull knobs are broken. That will do, boys."

We secured the boards and, along with two other dockhands, hoisted the container. The worn boards of the wagon bed squeaked and cracked under the weight of the Wurlitzer, but managed to support it. I couldn't help but wonder if the organ's bench would support Mrs. Adamson as she played the Wurlitzer at her fancy parties.

"Mr. Hunt wanted to make sure you remembered there was a delivery charge, Mrs. Adamson," I said, figuring I'd rather have her refuse, if she was going to, before we went through the work of actually delivering it.

"A delivery charge? Why, of all the nerve." Mrs. Adamson plowed her way through the two men who'd helped us load the freight. "I agreed to no such terms, young man. Don't you know who I am? This is absurd and unacceptable." By this time her face was red beneath her salt and pepper hair.

Where the calmness came from, I don't know, but I simply reached down and pulled out the invoice. "I'm sure a lady of your stature remembers that your signature accompanied your consent to pay a delivery charge." Mrs. Adamson snatched the paper from my hand and intently read the conditions of delivery.

"It has been over six months since you ordered it, Mrs. Adamson. It's a legitimate oversight to not remember the fine print," I said.

She thrust the paper back at me, "Yes, an oversight. That's all." She slapped the horse. "We've wasted enough time on this nonsense," she said. "Now, follow me." She mounted her horse with the agility of a drunken logger, then bullied her way past the merchants dock workers. We followed, keeping our distance and with our heads lowered. Of course her continued remarks shattered any hope of anonymity.

Mrs. Adamson's belligerence wasn't without its causes. In 1906, two years after the paper had started publication, Mrs. Adamson found herself the target of gossip and slander in St. Maries. It was fall of that year, and most of the summer dances and festivities had come and gone. Mrs. Adamson had been sick throughout the summer with rheumatism, missing her opportunity to socialize and flaunt her position among the townspeople. Since she had the means, she hosted a dinner and dance at the St. Maries Hotel. The evening had all of the makings of a successful celebration: a band was brought up from Coeur d' Alene; the liquor cabinet was stocked; the hotel kitchen had been working on the menu all week; and the weather looked like it was going to cooperate. She had her husband dedicate a half-page of the Sunday edition to the event, hoping to draw people from all over the county. On the day of the gala, the whole town was buzzing, deciding what to wear and arguing over who was courting who. Men were strutting in starched shirts, shined boots, and greased-back hair; women pranced around the streets in bonnets, corsets and flowing dresses; children wandered about, polite and attentive, knowing if they reverted to playground behavior, they'd sure as hell get a whipping.

The festivities started just as the sun was settling for the night. Mrs. Adamson made her appearance on the porch of the hotel, decorated more ornately than the community Christmas tree in December. She was wearing a deep green gown, covered with lace, and had a parasol that matched. Each finger had its own ring, and her neck was weighted with gold and silver strands hung with pendants and lockets. It was clear that the belle of the ball had arrived.

"Ladies and gentlemen," she started, "thank you for coming this evening to what is clearly the event of the year. It brings me great pleasure to welcome you to this grand showing of hospitality." You could almost hear the swish of everyone's rolling eyes, but they'd tolerate the pomp and arrogance for the sake of the evening. The crowd responded with courteous applause. "Before we get started, I will present a poem I have written for the occasion." She reached into a nearby bag and brought out a scroll of parchment that rolled out to nearly a man's height. "It's titled, 'An Evening In Fall,' by Louise Adamson." Just as she started reading, the clang of the fire station bell broke through. The crowd came alive, knowing that if it wasn't their own property burning, it would certainly be that of someone they knew. Mrs. Adamson tried to regain attention, but a runner was making his way in and out of the wagons that lined Main Street. Once he was within shouting distance, he jumped on top of a nearby wagon bed. The young man tried to catch his breath, spitting out bits and pieces of what had happened. Handy, who was nearby, jumped up next to him, and interpreted, "It's da Goldwyn home—kitch'n fiare is out of control!"

Mr. and Mrs. Goldwyn, along with their two sons, bolted from the back of the crowd. They were followed by the skeleton-crew that made up the volunteer fire department. And as the remaining crowd breathed a sigh of relief, each on knew that they should respond by helping fight the fire. Granted, the Goldwyns were new to town and hadn't been the most neighborly, but a common bond of ownership and camaraderie was part of living in St. Maries, especially in times of crisis. The smoke from the blaze started to appear on the dimly lit horizon. Handy continued atop the wagon bed.

"I'll sup'ly da buckets from my shop—hail, da home is less than 1,000 feet or so from da river, and we can get a brigade goin' in no time if we git our ass a movin'. We can use every'un, ladies 'n chilren alike." That's all that was needed. The crowd made its way by foot, wagon and horseback down Main Street to lend a hand. Everyone, that is, except Mrs. Adamson.

"Stop! I demand that everyone stop!" she shouted from the hotel porch. A few people within spitting distance slowed down, but for the most part, nobody paid her a lick of attention. Even her husband was stripping off his jacket and tie. Mrs. Adamson was at her wits' end, imprisoned by pride, selfishness and social standing, thinking of her spoiled evening and the realization that she was going to be upstaged by a family that didn't even exist in her eyes. Finally, in desperation, she yelled as only she could, "Damn, you people. You'd rather help out a bunch of Jews than attend my gala—may you rot in hell!"

A pregnant pause swept over the remaining crowd and the moment stood stagnant. Still engrossed in her rage, Louise Adamson didn't seem to have heard what she said, so she just stood there, poised as a peacock. Mr. Adamson quickly grabbed her by the arm and pulled her into the front door of the hotel, hoping to avoid any further embarrassment. Handy returned and recaptured the attention of the rest of the townspeople by shooting off a 30-30 rifle.

"Thit fiare is still mighty hungry. Let's git goin'!" He whipped the horses and led the stragglers toward the fire. Thanks to the participation of the community, the Goldwyns suffered minimal damage. What's more, they were so taken by the expression of goodwill, they made a sizable contribution to the city for the purchase of a new pumping wagon.

Since it took less than three hours to contain the fire, the evening was still young when the fire fighting ended. Mrs. Adamson had long since gone home, so Mr. Adamson, who had pitched in with the rest of us, asked the hotel to setup the food on the porch because of the soot covering those who'd been on the front lines and the mud and water that bogged down the rest. The band played from the upstairs balcony overlooking the street. Steel barrels were brought in from around town and filled with firewood for make-shift fireplaces. Families stayed well into the night, dancing, singing and eating to their hearts' content.   It was the best time ever remembered in St. Maries.

The week following the event, The Gazette printed a letter, penned by Mrs. Adamson, apologizing for the remarks made in a "brief lapse of discretion."   It was a poor repentance but was accepted by the Goldwyns and a good part of the community. I remembered how Ollie had showed us where Mr. Hunt had framed and hung the article in his office, saying if Louise Adamson ever needed a dose of who she really was, he'd be glad to assist her in remembering.

●   ●   ●   ●   ●

The Adamson home sat above a grove of poplars, with a half-dozen or so rooted just outside their front room.   Their place was flanked by mountains and fronted by a breath-taking view of the St. Joe valley. It was truly spectacular. I started backing up to the front porch, which had a section of railing removed to give us easy access to the music room, which was just off of the entry way.   Once again Mrs. Adamson was an expeditious help.

"Don't mess it up now, young man, or you'll be working until Christ's return to pay for this thing," she said.

Mrs. Adamson went into the house to clear a place for the Wurlitzer, giving us a brief yet appreciated reprieve. We pulled some peeled cedar poles from the wagon, laid them down, and proceeded to jockey the crate onto them.

"It sure is easier to use your brains than your brawn isn't it, Drew?" I said.

"I don't know, J.D. I'm more inclined toward a good grunt and lift than all of this fuss over an easy way to move things."

Drew had been consistently subdued since that morning, appearing to be bothered by any unneeded conversation. We rolled the instrument to the threshold, where we uncrated it. Once Mrs. Adamson had changed her mind five times, we finally moved the Wurlitzer into place.

When she was satisfied she told us to come in so she could settle accounts. We followed her through the house, past the formal living room, the dining room, the sitting room and finally into Mr. Adamson's office. It had a roll-top desk in the far corner that was strewn with clippings and notes layered on top of photographs and recent past editions of the Gazette. The mess spilled onto a table next to the desk. Mrs. Adamson rummaged through the desk, looking for a bottle of ink.

"I have a quill in my bag," she said. "Wait here and I'll be right back.

The stairs complained under her feet. Drew and I started to look around the room, biding our time while Mrs. Adamson moved from room to room as the floors creaked above us. There was a telegram from Spokane about the Union Pacific Railroad establishing a distribution hub there, a commentary on the mining industry and the destructive procedures used to glean precious minerals, an obituary from a family over in Harrison, and a report from the Forest Service with the latest fire danger figures.   For the most part, it was far from captivating.   Then, I noticed Drew was fixed on a journal open on the table in front of him.

"What do you have there?" I asked.

"Shhh!" Drew was concentrating. I hurried to peer over his shoulder.

"What is it?" I asked.

Drew lifted the cover so I could see the front as he continued to read. "Investigative Leads," was scribbled in pencil. He set the cover back down and I read with him:

> *Received   more   reports   of*
> *commotion at the Schrag house.*
> *Decided to see for myself— asked*
> *a few questions of "A" sources.*
> *1) reports of screaming from*
> *children - heard it myself.*

*2) no one knows where he goes to
make his money
3) has been seen over in Kellogg
with convicted horse thieves
4) reports of theft and missing
livestock increasing*

The stairs signaled Mrs. Adamson's return. Drew and I tried our best to look innocent when she walked in, but she was so engrossed in her own dealings that she probably wouldn't have noticed if we were editing the stories ourselves. She signed the invoice and paid the bill, complete with delivery charges.

"Here you are, $503.00 even. You and your friend can keep the extra." Quite an expression of gratitude, considering the bill came to $502.80. Drew and I climbed aboard the wagon and made our way back to the mercantile.

"Do you reckon Schrag's doing some shady business in Kellogg, J.D.?" Drew asked.

"Drew, we have no way of proving that and you know it. Besides, it's not for us to be concerned about."

"Jackson, Anna and those boys have to live with him. How can you say that doesn't concern me?"

"I guess I can't, Drew." We continued the rest of the way back to the mercantile in silence, since he didn't want to tell me what he figured on doing and to be honest, I didn't want to know.

Chapter 10

The rest of the week continued like any other, besides the anticipation of our journey. Even Ollie, who acted as though the imminent adventure didn't frighten him, was showing signs of nervousness.

"Are the three of you attending church this weekend?" Phoebe asked as Drew, Ollie and I were walking from the schoolhouse. It was Friday and attending church wasn't high on our agenda for the weekend. Still, Phoebe had been asking since the beginning of the year, when her pastor had offered to dedicate a special service to the five of us. He did it for every graduating class, but this year would be special because he liked Phoebe so well. We couldn't avoid giving her an answer anymore, since the service was only two days away.

"I'll be there, Phoebe," Ollie said, which was no exercise of will, since he attended every week.

"I'll be there, too," I said. "Someone has to keep Ollie in line."

Drew paused. He'd never been much of a churchgoer, so I reckoned that he was a bit intimidated by the proposition. "Can Anna come along, too?"

"Of course, Andrew—everyone's welcome." Phoebe never missed a chance to invite people to her church. "The service is at 10:00 a.m. sharp," she said. "I'll see you then."

Phoebe left smiling. "She'll probably make us sit in the front row, ya know," Ollie said.

"What's wrong with that?" I asked.

"I don't know, it's sort of like an up close portrait of God. Besides, it makes me squirm when Reverend Turlick has that close an eye on me."

"You just don't like the fact that you'll have to stay awake the whole time."

We laughed as we made our way toward the river. Since it was Friday, we didn't have to work.

"I reckon it won't hurt to spend some time with God just before our trip, anyhow," Ollie said. Then he asked me about supplies for the trip. I reached into my pocket and pulled out a folded up piece of paper on which I'd been keeping a running list.

"A cured ham and two slabs of bacon from Drew's kin; each of us bringing our own bedrolls, fishing gear and clothes; my folks are supplying the cooking utensils; and your folks are lettin' us borrow the horses. Other than the dry goods and a few things like matches and such that we'll be getting from the mercantile, that about does it." I folded the list and started to put it back in my pocket, when Ollie stopped me.

"J.D., you forgot one very important item—
get that list back out." I unfolded it got ready to
write.

"Chaw," he said.

"What?" Drew and I chorused.

"Chaw. You gotta put that on your list.
What in sam-hell would a trip into God's country be
without a wad of chaw to flavor it? A good plug will
go a long way, so I reckon one will do us. Who's
gonna pick that up?"

"So we can get up there and puke?" Drew
was obviously unimpressed. In grammar school,
Drew's uncle had caught him with a full pocket of
the stuff. Though Drew swore he'd only been given
it by a friend and hadn't tried any, his uncle made
him put the whole wad in his mouth, saying if he
was going to chew tobacco it was as good a time to
start as any. Drew tried to spit, but his mouth was so
full that he swallowed most of it. He ended up
heaving the tobacco out along with most of his
dinner, and spent the remainder of the evening
doubled over in pain.

"Take it easy, big man. It was just a
suggestion." Ollie backed down but didn't retreat
completely. "I'll bring some for myself," he said.

As we neared the river, the horns from
riverboats filled the air, signaling their final run
down the St. Joe to Harrison and Coeur d' Alene.

The Georgie Oaks pulled her walkway up, a sign that she was full, leaving the Spokane to accommodate the rest of the passengers. People scurried to make the gate, knowing that if the Spokane left without them, they'd be stuck in St. Maries until the next day. The ferries were done for the week and there was only one run on Saturday and Sunday. Two men, well dressed enough to be lawyers, calmly approached the line of anxious people pushing toward the boat and passed them, heading for a side entrance. They paid an inflated fare and walked aboard while the rest of the crowd continued to jockey for position.

From our vantage point on the walkway above the docks, the sea of people was a glimpse of wider society. The elderly were elbowed and shoved to the outside of the crowd, until a concerned soul let them in; a woman with children was treated more like a nuisance than a customer; the strong overpowered the weak; pretty ladies were given leeway while the homely ones were left to fend for themselves.

When the Spokane had completed its boarding, everyone who had wanted to had somehow gotten on board. The whistle blew, steam bellowed from the stacks, and the paddle wheel churned the floating mass downstream.

"Bet the hotel is mad no one got left behind,"
Ollie said.   "I heard the owners tried to buy the
Spokane just so they could limit the number of
passengers."   This would be gossip from the
mercantile, which was rarely accurate and frequently
turned out to be outright lies.

With the riverboats on their way, we quickly
lost interest in the docks, so we continued our hike
along the river. At the city limits, Main Street veered
south and we took a wagon trail that followed the
river banks. The trail was used to access logs that got
loose from their floats. This year it was well worn
because the water was so low. Timber was more apt
to catch on the bank or on shallow snags.

We walked along in silence, enjoying the
river sounds. The slow current lapped at the rocky
shores, so that we fell into pace with its rhythm. An
occasional fish would rise, making a flipping sound
and sending circles out, which quickly dissipated as
they got larger, and silent water skippers skimmed
the river, undoubtedly eyed by trout beneath the
water's surface.

At its headwaters above Avery, the St. Joe is
nothing more than a stream, but 127 miles down
river the water is deep when it runs into Lake Coeur
d' Alene. The highest navigable river in the world,
the St. Joe is also one of the few whose banks actually
run through a lake. From a vista atop Harrison

Ridge, you can distinctly see the St. Joe River, flanked on either side by Lake Chatcolet and Benewah Lake, as it makes it way toward Lake Coeur d' Alene, a strange sight that has kept geologists and historians guessing to this day about how it was created. Add to all of this the uncharted territory that the river wound through and for Drew, Ollie, and me, you have the precise reason our minds were set on our trip to Avery.

We stopped at the meadow at Johnson's Bend, reclined our backs, and soaked our feet in the cool water while the sun's rays sparkled off the river's surface.

"Do you think it's sissy to like beauty?" Drew asked.

"What kind of question is that?" Ollie said.

Drew's face flushed. "I don't know. Maybe I'm wondering if I'm, you know, normal."

"Let me put your mind at rest, Drew—you're not!"

I glared at Ollie. "It's perfectly normal, Drew. What do you find beautiful?"

Drew folded his arms across his chest. "Lots of things, I guess."

Ollie persisted. "Something specific must come to mind. You're the one who brought it up."

"There isn't any one thing, alright?" Drew said, irritated. Both Ollie and I knew there was something on his mind, but sure as hell Ollie's tactics were only going to get him a whipping.

"I think what Ollie means is what kind of things do you think have beauty?"

"Simple things," he said. "Like a new born deer, or a fresh cut red fir, or the Georgie Oaks' reflection as she heads up river."

"Miss Sorensen cooking me my breakfast, wearing nothing more than an apron and a smile." Ollie added.

"That's fantasy, Ollie," I said.

"The hell it is! To a man any less it may be, but I'd guess my virility surpasses even my own estimations. Miss Sorensen is putty in my hands."

Drew chuckled and I shook my head. "Your own estimations are all you got, I'd say. And they're unencumbered by reality to boot."

I reckon Drew wasn't sure what "unencumbered" meant, but he knew I'd slammed Ollie with it, which was enough for him.

"What about you, J.D.?" he asked.

"Everyday words. An open camp fire." I figured I knew where the whole conversation was coming from. "You thinking about Anna, Drew?" I asked.

"More like she *is* beauty. Her smile—I swear I damn near pissed my pants the first time she flashed it at me. Yes sir, Anna Schrag is beauty

Red River Valley, The Old Rugged Cross, Amazing Grace and other favorite folk songs and hymns. Drew and I joined in when we knew the words. And although I could hold my own when it came to singing, Drew had the volume and pitch of a foghorn. He would coast along half a beat behind singing the same three notes over and over. Mrs. Hunt would say that the Lord hears a perfect voice when we sing so Drew's singing was evidently a melodious offering to Him. Ollie would remind her that here on Earth we are confined to our human limitations and that Drew's singing was more like a penance than an offering. On this particular hot afternoon it didn't matter who the virtuoso was because the sound of the mauls drowned out any musical inaccuracies. Mrs. Hunt came in with some iced tea that had been brewing all afternoon.

"You boys are thirsty, I reckon. Sit down and relax a spell." She poured tea over cubed ice, which crackled and snapped in the warm liquid. We pulled up empty crates and tamarack rounds to sit on, grabbing eagerly for the tea.

"Don't drink too fast or you'll stomach will disagree with you" she said. The cool liquid felt good on our throats, which were coated with flour dust. "How much more do you have?"

"We should have it knocked out inside an hour if we hump," Mr. Hunt said. I wanted to groan.

My muscles were stiffening and my fingers were bleeding from poking them one too many times with the sack-sewing needle. It must have shown on my face.

"Are you sure you're not working these boys too hard, Franklin?" Mrs. Hunt asked.

"Too hard? They're eighteen years old. If they can't handle a few hours hard labor, they aren't ready to be released in to this world. I'm doing them a favor by giving them a taste of real work."

I wished Mr. Hunt hadn't been so convincing, but Mrs. Hunt filled our glasses one last time and started to gather up all she'd brought. "I'll need one of the boys to help me in a little while," she said. "I have a few things that need rearranging. I'll holler when I'm ready." As she headed back each of us hoped Mr. Hunt would choose us. Even Ollie looked willing, despite his distaste for rearranging.

After what seemed hours, the grain sacks were all but finished. We had filled a dozen and a half sacks of flour, enough to last ten graduations. Mrs. Hunt reappeared. "Franklin, which one of these boys can I take?" she asked.

"Jackson, you go ahead and I'll finish sewing up these last few sacks. Andrew and Oliver can finish bagging what we've crushed," Mr. Hunt said. I handed off my sewing needle, trying not to look too grateful.

"Bring in two flour sacks with you, Jackson. We'll sell them out in no time."

I shouldered the sacks and followed Mrs. Hunt, who told me to fill the bins and leave the rest of the sack next to the counter so she could top them off later.

Mrs. Hunt was a meticulous woman. If a product came in that she hadn't carried before, Mrs. Hunt would rearrange everything to accommodate it. That's what drove Ollie crazy. He'd simply set the item down on the floor next to a stack of other goods, but Mrs. Hunt would argue that they weren't grouped properly, or that their sizes weren't proportionate. It was the kind of attitude that irritated less particular types like Ollie and me. But it beat crushing cracked wheat any day. I finished the flour and waiting for me was another chore, then another, and another.

"You're a good worker, Jackson," Mrs. Hunt said. "Why don't you let some of that rub off on Ollie? He could use a dose or two."

"Ollie and work don't go too well together, Mrs. Hunt. I'm sure you know that by now."

"Yes, I suppose I do—unless it has something to do with fishing."

"That's for sure."

"How do you and Andrew put up with him? I'd figure the two of you would tire of his lip and laziness?"

I worked at restacking a shelf of canned goods. "Ollie, he's valuable for in . . . intang . . ."

"Intangible?"

"That's the word. For his intangible qualities. He's like color on a plain canvas."

"That's well said, Jackson."

"Not to say he doesn't chap me when he's sitting around expecting everyone else to pick up the slack, but more often than not he's a good guy to have around."

Mrs. Hunt paused, looking out at Main Street. "That about nails it, Jackson. He's a good guy to have around. I suppose that's a reminder to me that I need to appreciate him for what he is and not persecute him for what he isn't." She broke a smile then said, "But why, in the name of all that's sacred, did the good Lord make him my oldest? My luck he'll set suit for his brother and sisters to follow and I'll have a house full of colorful canvases and no one to do any work."

Ollie knew why he frustrated his mother, and he enjoyed taunting her. He'd exaggerate his reaction to topics, predominantly religious. His mom might say something about the importance of celibacy before marriage, and Ollie might respond that maybe this waiting thing wasn't all it was cracked up to be. Aghast, his mom would mutter some prayer about God having mercy on her son's ignorance. It was a game of sorts, and one I think she enjoyed as well as he did.

The slam of the mercantile door startled us both. I turned, but from my position at the back of the store all I could see was a man in a straw hat flanked by some young ones and a lady. He walked toward us, caulked boots tearing at the floorboards.

"Please remove your boots," Mrs. Hunt called. "You're welcome but your boots aren't."

The man didn't break stride down the grocery aisles toward the counter where Mrs. Hunt was standing. Her face grew tight as he approached. The lady and children waited at the store entrance. I stepped down from my stool and joined Mrs. Hunt at the counter.

"Sir, maybe you didn't hear me, but please remove your boots—they're ruining my floor," she said.

By this time he was nearly to the counter and Mrs. Hunt was nervously shifting her weight from one foot to the other. I slid behind the counter and positioned myself abreast of Mrs. Hunt, putting the counter between me and the advancing man. It wasn't until he was all but at the counter that I recognized him—Anna's dad, Batum Schrag. My blood froze. I was useless.

Mrs. Hunt took a deep breath. "Batum, your inconsiderate behavior will get you nowhere in this store."

The stench of alcohol arrived a good five feet before he did. His glossy eyes and stuttered steps affirmed: he was drunk. Mrs. Hunt glared. He leaned on the counter and pulled a wad of paper from the pocket of his braced pants. "I need some goods."

Mrs. Hunt went up on her toes so she could lean over and get in his face. "If it weren't for your family, I wouldn't give you the time of day, Mr. Schrag."

Batum smiled a smart-ass grin and proceeded to spread the list out on the counter in front of him. Then in a rasped voice he said, "I don't want the time of day lady, just the goods."

Mrs. Hunt snatched the list from the counter and handed it to me. "Fill the man's list, Jackson, so he can be on his way."

The feeling returned to my legs and I scurried around the store filling the order. The family at the front of the store turned out to be Anna and her brothers. When she saw me, she herded the boys out onto the front porch to sit on some fruit crates. She turned toward the street and sat with her arms around them. I gathered the last of the items, boxed them and then placed the box on the counter in front of Anna's dad.

"That'll be $4.37," Mrs. Hunt said after adding it up on her ledger. Batum pulled out a dollar bill and some loose change.

"I reckon I can pay at least half now and the rest on my next trip to town."

"You don't have credit here, Mr. Schrag."

"The hell I don't." he shouted. "I lived in St. Maries long before you corn-huskers came to town."

Mrs. Hunt replied, "You've been drinking that long, too, which means you waste more money in a weekend than the total of this box of goods. As I've told you before, when feeding your family becomes more important than a shot of rye-whiskey, you come in here and I'll extend you some credit. Not until then."

Just then, Drew entered from the kitchen. "Mrs. Hunt, your husband said you might be needin' another sack of flour," his voice trailing off.

"Just set it down by the bin, Andrew," Mrs. Hunt said, keeping her eyes on Batum.

"Is everything alright?" Drew asked, coming over to stand by me.

"What'll it be Mr. Schrag? You've got $1.74. Can you decide what you need most or shall I?"

Batum dropped his eyes for a moment, then peered out from below the brim of his tattered hat. "The day I need some wench to make up my mind is the day you'll see my balls hangin' from a tree."

"Get your filthy mouth out of this store."

"When I have my goods."

"That's no longer a possibility. From now on, if your family needs something, you send Anna over to get it."

Batum stood up from his slouched position on the counter and cocked his arm back. His drunkenness gave Drew enough time to bolt around the counter and intercept the blow. Mrs. Hunt backed up against the shelves behind the counter then whispered to me, "Run out and get Franklin!"

"When Mrs. Hunt says you're not welcome, I reckon you ought to listen," Drew said.

Batum jerked his hand loose and squared off. "So the big dumb one thinks he's going to step in?"

"I don't want any trouble, sir. I just think you better head on home."

"The second you lay hands on me you got trouble, son."

Batum motioned as if he were leaving, and then turned back, catching Drew off guard and cocked him up side the head. Drew fell into a table of cans and a basket of produce. Mrs. Hunt screamed as Batum advanced toward Drew. Anna burst in through the front door as Mr. Hunt entered through the back, wielding the axe handle he'd been using to crush the wheat.

"One more step, Batum, and I'll send your head rolling along with those apples." Mr. Hunt said.

"I was just teaching the little bastard a lesson."

Anna stood just a few feet away. Batum looked over at her. "Get your ass up here and get us some goods—everything on that list." With that he turned and made his way past Anna out of the store. Anna stepped up to the counter without looking up. She signed for the goods. Mrs. Hunt reached across the counter and put her hand on Anna's cheek.

"You know there's a God who cares for you. It may not feel like it at times, but He's hurting with you."

Anna looked up to Mrs. Hunt through her tears. "Yes ma'am."

Ollie and I helped Drew to his feet. Anna stopped with her box of goods just before passing Drew. Without looking at him she said, "Are you alright, Andrew?"

"Yeah, Anna," he said. "I'll be fine."

She sighed and continued out the door. We watched Anna and her brothers load into the back of the wagon and head down Main Street with Batum Schrag in the lead.

Drew rubbed the side of his face. "I reckon Anna and the boys won't rest until that man's six feet under . . . and 'm not sure I will, either."

Chapter 12

(North Idaho, Fall, 1979) Lenny's eyes were starting to droop, his head was nodding. He tried to maintain an interest, but the clock was striking midnight. Still chewing on parched corn, J.D. was slowing as well. He wiped the pan with the grease-spotted newspaper and looked up at the rusty old clock.

"Hell, it's late. If I don't get some sleep tonight, I'll be as stopped up as a bear during hibernation."

Lenny smiled, a bit embarrassed, but nodded in agreement.

They doused what was left of the fire and made their way out the door. "You have a mind for detail, in woodworking and story telling, J.D.," Lenny commented.

He reset his locking contraption, sealing the shop. "Well they both come natural, but I can't make a nickel off either of them."

"You never sold your furniture?"

"Naw, we would have starved if we'd relied on my woodworking. My daddy taught it to me when I was growing up. It used to get me out of the house so I wouldn't drive the missus crazy. But now that she's not here, I'm more apt to be inside where she used to be than out in the shop."

Lenny was sorry he asked, as he could tell J.D. still thought of his wife, the way Lenny did his. Divorce and death are like that. They take everything but recollection from you.

"Yep, I went to college and got my degree in English Literature," J.D. said. "That's where I met my wife."

"I didn't know you had a degree."

"Didn't use it for a while. After graduate school, the Mrs. and I moved back here and I worked with my brother and father in the woods until the end of World War II. Taught at the University in Moscow after that, then retired and moved back here. My pension and Social Security are plenty these days."

He tossed me the keys to his pickup. "You up for a start around six o'clock?" he asked. "The windshield wipers only work when it's not raining, but she runs great." His four teeth shone and the wrinkles on his face doubled as he smiled.

Lenny thought of J.D., returning to St. Maries after earning a Master's degree in English and then returning again to retire. What he knew of commitment had just faded into a bad memory, except for his children. And a stranger was teaching him about the heritage he didn't know existed.

Grandma's house was dark and silent when Lenny pulled into the driveway, the path to her front porch lit only by a bare bulb hanging from the eves. He slipped in the front door and found the couch made up for his bed. His feet were barely under the covers when he fell asleep.

•   •   •   •   •

In the morning, Lenny stumbled to the breakfast table. "How was your time with Jackson, Lenny?" mom asked.

"I spent the night eating myself in to oblivion and listening to stories."

"Loretta called this morning. She said the kids are fine." Mom fidgeted with her coffee spoon. "She asked how you were doing."

Lenny's stomach tightened as his face turned flush. You don't expect a marriage to fail, and then it does. He probably should have seen it coming, at least that's what his wife Loretta said. All he knew was that a divorce doesn't just happen; it lingers.

"Well, I'm doing great. Just great." He slurped his coffee.

"She seemed concerned. Maybe she wants to talk."

"Don't, Mom. We're divorced. She cares about me as long as she doesn't have to do anything about it," Lenny barked. He put down his coffee cup.

Mom had tilted her head away from him. He took a deep breath and hushed his voice.

"Mom, the marriage is over."

Mom looked up, her eyes were wet. "I guess I don't want to admit that."

Lenny hugged her and grabbed his jacket. "I'm heading back to J.D.'s. We have a few supplies to get. If everything goes as planned, we should be done with the fence by early tomorrow afternoon." He twisted the door handle. "Everything will be alright," he said. She smiled faintly as the door shut behind him.

●   ●   ●   ●   ●

J.D. was coming out his front door when Lenny pulled up to his house.

"I thought we'd take a trip up to St. Joe City, just a few miles up the St. Joe River," J.D. said as he hoisted himself into the passenger seat. "A friend of mine has a small mill up there. He'll give me a good deal on the fence boards." Lenny backed out of the driveway and headed back toward Main Street.

"St. Joe City. The first stop on your trip to Avery?"

"You're listening better than I figured you were, Lenny Dougherty. Yep, that is where we got off the barge and started on the first leg of our journey."

"After graduation, right?"

"Uh-huh. We showed up in St. Joe City right after commencement, 1910. Now there's a conundrum. They call it a 'commencement' but the kids think it's an end, not a beginning. For the longest time, I thought the word meant 'to finish,' just because of graduation. It wasn't until I saw my first automobile that I understood."

Lenny smiled faintly, as if he knew what an automobile had to do with the subject at hand.

"You know," he said. "A commencer—the crank we used to start an automobile before electric starters were invented."

"Oh. Right," Lenny said.

"I finally deduced there's no way commence could mean 'the end' if, in fact, it meant to start an automobile, but then why the hell would they use it to signify the end of a person's high school education?" J.D. paused for a moment. "So what I finally came to terms with is that it means both. It's the end of the old and the beginning of the new." He smiled, too genuinely pleased with himself to seem arrogant.

On their trip up to St. Joe City, J.D. pointed out some of the original homesteads, where the Mercantile once stood, as well as Miller's Corner,

Handy's blacksmith shop, the St. Maries Hotel, and finally the pilings that once held the magnificent boardwalks along the river.

The road meandered to the outskirts of town, where they approached a small stone church with boards over the windows. The sign, which was still somewhat legible, read, "St. Maries Community Chapel. Peter Turlick, Minister."

"Pull over here, Lenny."

The two got out of the truck in the middle of an overgrown yard. The doors were made of pine boards whose glue had cracked. J.D. pulled hard and they opened, creaking on their rusted hinges. The morning sun streamed through the decayed roof, illuminating most of the room. Chimney bricks were scattered around the oil stove, and the rafters, made of rough-cut four-by-tens, sagged under the weight of the old roof. The building's rock foundation was showing its age, too. The entire church listed to one side. The cross mounted on the wall, however, stood perfectly erect.

"Kind of a queer sight, ain't it?" J.D. asked.

"The cross? I noticed."

"I reckon your granddad would've said it's because we're in God's country.

"I bet Ollie would've had something to say about that."

"He'd have laughed. It wasn't like him to miss a chance to poke fun."

A damp, cool wind rustled through the church roof. "And what angle would a young Jackson Donner have taken?" Lenny asked.

"A combination of the two, I suppose. Ollie always spoke a worldly truth and your granddaddy, well, he spoke an intuitive one."

J.D. wandered up to the pulpit, which was covered with a layer of dust and pigeon droppings. "Revered Turlick had a special message for us the Sunday we graduated. He spoke on hell. Same thing he said to every graduating class. Hell was a day without the smell of an evergreen—and since the rains hadn't come that spring, it reminded us we needed to be on the watch for fire. He called it Satan's tool, the demon fire."

"I suppose that's just about right, in these parts."

"The forest was our lifeline, even more so than it is now. We didn't know anything else."

A pigeon fluttered through the roof and perched on a rafter. "Was it a good sermon?"

J.D. smiled. "I don't know if Reverend Turlick ever preached a good sermon. They always ended with an altar call no one responded to, and you could set your calendar by his themes. But the town liked him enough that he baptized, married and buried the population a dozen times over."

Some of the pews were still intact while others had been taken or vandalized and lay in splintered heaps on the wood-plank floor. Lenny joined J.D. at the pulpit. J.D. set his hand on the front pew and lowered himself to a sitting position.

"I sat here that day," he said. "Phoebe sat next to me on my right, with your granddad and Anna on my left. Drew was so nervous he hugged the arm of the pew like it was his last will and testament. Ollie sat next to Phoebe and Isabel next to him." J.D. looked around. "It was quite a sight, each boy in a suit borrowed from his dad, so oversized that when we sat down the shoulders came up to our ears." He cackled, delighted. "Mrs. Farnsworth, the church piano player, sat just to the right of Reverend Turlick. On a good day you could recognize the tune she was playing, let alone sing along. I'm not sure if it was her fault or because the town's piano tuner was deaf in one ear." He laughed again, but this time quieter, as if to keep from disturbing his surroundings. "'Tis so sweet to trust in Jesus' . . . that's the song we sang that day. Ollie knew all the words . . . he and Phoebe both. The rest of us . . . we just fumbled along." J.D.'s voice trailed off into a whisper. "Can't say that I remember any more of the song . . . Ollie knew it, though . . . yes he surely did."

Lenny stood there watching, J.D. now completely unaware of his presence. He continued to whisper the words to the old hymn, this time just shy of being entirely inaudible. His eyes focused at the front of the church. He smiled momentarily, but then it faded from his mouth, his eyes glossed over with tears, his head shook slowly from side to side.

Chapter 13

The pickup truck crossed over the St. Joe River just east of town, below the river's confluence with the St. Maries River. The bridge took them to the river's north side, the road winding along its shadowy banks. Small tributaries dotted the route, cascading down the mountain on their left. The morning was crisp and Lenny took in as much of it as he could.

The St. Joe River was every bit as beautiful as J.D. had described. Lenny had traveled the same road more than a dozen times as a child, but never noticed the brilliance of the river from the back seat of his family's Rambler station wagon. Marshy fields lined the flats, with pussy willows poking through a light haze over the water. J.D. broke in.

"When the Forest Service finally built a road to Avery in '29, it followed in and out of every draw. I reckon it took eight hours to make the trip from St. Maries. These days it's just shy of two hours. It took the engineering genius of the 1960s to finally figure a way to levy this road so the floods wouldn't destroy it every year."

The old road that J.D. described could occasionally be seen peeking around the edge of the hills and then heading back into the innermost parts of the draws. It was easy to see how it could have taken a day's driving to negotiate.

"In fact," J.D. continued, "I received my first driving lesson on that road, right after World War I. My daddy bought a surplussed army truck and converted it for logging. I reckon I ground off a hundred miles worth of gears in one trip. But I learned how to drive all the same." J.D. peered out his window. "But that was a different time, Lenny Dougherty, a different time."

Lenny tried to imagine what J.D. saw out his window: turn of the century automobiles navigating dusty streets; rugged men and hard women struggling to eke out a living; large families with small pantries.

"It's a grand song, you know?" J.D.'s voice startled Lenny.

"What is?"

"The commencement march played at graduation. Every time I hear it my face warms and tingles rush down my spine. Daa-da-da-daa--daa-da-da-daa--daa-da-da-daa-daaa . . . the five of us, donned with homemade gowns and caps fresh from the Sears and Roebuck catalog, were ready to make our mark on society. And a hell of a mark we made."

Lenny thought of J.D. in a homemade cap and gown and five graduating seniors parading down the aisle. "That must have been the shortest 'Pomp and Circumstance' ever played," he said. "Did they even get past the introduction?"

"The band played fast and we walked slow—with a good ten yards between each of us. It sounded terrible, so it was probably a good thing it was short. I reckon the audience wouldn't have lasted if we had a sixth person in our class. They only stuck around because the St. Maries Hotel hosted a dance that spilled into the street and lasted to the early hours of the morning. It was a grand time." J.D. fell silent for a few minutes. It appeared postcards from the past were cluttering his mind again. "There wasn't any trouble that evening, but it was quick on our heels."

Lenny listened intently, guiding J.D.'s truck along the banks of the St. Joe River toward the mill at St. Joe City, where his adventure had begun almost a century before.

•   •   •   •   •

(June, 1910) Miss Sorensen released us from class early that Friday, knowing our minds were focused on the approaching graduation ceremony. All of our final assignments had been graded and a year's worth of exams were returned to us along with our respective scores. Phoebe finished at the top of our class, then Ollie and Isabel, followed by me and then Drew.

Drew was able to convince Miss Sorensen to let Anna go early as well, seeing as how she was next year's leader and could benefit from keeping our company. Miss Sorensen said she figured Anna could teach us a thing or two in the way of manners and decency, and conceded to let her go along. Our first stop was Miller's Corner.

"We're back for more punishment, Mr. Miller," Ollie said, scattering a handful of change on the counter. "With cash this time."

"It's a good thing, Oliver, considering your parents informed me your credit is only as good as your word." Mr. Miller was as serious as he could be.

"Will you be there tonight, Mr. Miller?" Isabel asked.

"I wouldn't miss it." Mr. Miller lined up the fountain glasses across the freshly wiped counter. "And who is your friend? I don't recall her being with you last time."

Drew peered up sheepishly at Mr. Miller. "This here is Anna—she's with me."

"Yes, I figured she was, Andrew. It's nice to make your acquaintance, Anna." Mr. Miller leaned down and began scooping. "Are you sure you want to be involved with this bunch of hooligans?"

Anna's dark complexion flushed as she searched for an answer. "They're not so bad after you get to know them." Drew grabbed Anna's hand, her skin turned scarlet.

Mr. Miller smiled once again. "No, I guess they're not, save for a certain neighbor of mine."

"Who, me?" Ollie glanced around the room, pretending to search for the target of Mr. Miller's teasing.

Phoebe walked over and stood next to him. "If you weren't so adorable I'd think of you the same way, Oliver Hunt." With that Phoebe gave him a kiss on the cheek, and he matched Anna's shade.

"Are you gentlemen still planning to take off for Avery?" Mr. Miller asked, sliding each of us a bubbling soda.

"The barge leaves tomorrow at 2:00 p.m. for the mill." Ollie said, scooping at his overflowing soda. "Unless Jesus himself comes to get us, we'll be on that boat."

"Supplies are packed and horses ready, Mr. Miller," I said.

"And you, Mr. Featherweight. Are you as anxious to wander for nearly a month in the North Idaho wilderness?"

Drew hesitated with his hand still over Anna's. "Yes sir, I reckon I am. I can't get out of my mind that tall tamarack where your brother is buried. If I have my way, we're gonna find it, Mr. Miller."

"I'd be much obliged, Andrew."

Conversation moved from the advent of the automobile to the size of the biggest trout Ollie and Isabel had pulled from the St. Joe. Mr. Miller and Isabel talked about her future, and Phoebe listened to Ollie catalogue his accomplishments, what few of them there were. I simply observed, watching my friends' bodies communicate back and forth. Drew would only look at Anna when she spoke, and spent the rest of the time wringing his hands while he stared at the floor; Anna responded by gently touching his hands as if to relieve the anxiety coiled there. Mr. Miller gave Isabel fatherly looks, shaking his head and finger as he listed the benefits of a proper education. Phoebe and Ollie had moved to a table by the window. She kept attentive, even to his obnoxious hand gestures. They actually appeared to be enjoying each other's company. After seven years of teasing, bantering and taunting, it seemed they might be compatible—as compatible as a man and a woman could be.

We stepped back out into the afternoon sun and made our way toward the mercantile. Handy was in front of his shop as we approached, bent over a young colt.

"Sonabit'in thang. This here animal is gonna git it in the nougats if it steps on my feets one mo' time. I swear—"

"You certainly do," Phoebe said. "Enough for the whole town."

Handy looked up. His hat had fallen over his eyes and he was having a hell of a time peering out from under it. "Miss Phoebe and Miss Isabel, is that you?" Isabel snatched the hat off his head and gave him a whack with it.

"That's from Phoebe because of your foul mouth." Then she bent over and kissed his greasy forehead before putting the hat back in place. "And that's from me because of your foul mouth!" The girls giggled.

"You boys ain't laughin', is ya?" Handy dropped the colt's hoof and grabbed his tongs from the fire, brandishing them.

"No sir. We wouldn't laugh at another man's misery," Ollie said.

"Do I be seein' a grin on your mouth, little man?"

"Watch it there or I'll have to send my big friend after you." Try as he might, Ollie couldn't wipe the grin from his face.

"Mr. Fedderweight knows better than to mess wit a one-handed blacksmith who's got a set of red-hot ball crushers."

Phoebe and Isabel doubled over, enjoying every moment of Ollie's torment. Handy slapped the tongs across an anvil between him and Ollie, who escaped out the front door. Handy put the tongs back in the fire and pulled up a bucket to sit on. He broke a greasy smile, and then reached in his pocket for a pouch of tobacco and rolling papers. He pulled a paper out with his teeth, then sprinkled the tobacco onto the paper while it was in his mouth. Pulling the tobacco -covered paper out, he licked the edge quickly, then rolled the cigarette with his fingertips. Even one-handed, it was like one fluid motion. With his tongs, he took a burning ember from his fire to light up. "Two questions fer ya. Why are you buggin' me so early in the day, and who's the pretty addition to yer party?"

That time I think Drew blushed more than Anna. I guess she was getting used to it.

"This is Anna. She is a friend of Andrew's," Phoebe said.

"I thought I knew all da pretty uns. Does Anna have a last name?"

"Just Anna," Drew said. It startled all of us, including Anna.

The room was quiet a moment and then Phoebe asked Handy if he was coming to the ceremony.

"Let's see, would that be the belchin' contest at Haps or the gin bust at Nellie's?" Handy snickered.

"God have mercy on your soul!"

"Now don't get in a tizzy, Miss Phoebe. I wouldn't miss the five of you for all the horse shoes in Montana."

Phoebe broke a smile as big as Handy's. "I knew it. Seven p.m. sharp."

Handy puffed away at his cigarette and winked as we turned to leave. "The three of youse no-goods still plannin' on that trip to Avery?"

"Leaving tomorrow at 2:00," I said.

"Stop by here on yer way and I'll fine tune yer horse's shoes for the trip. Little graduatin' present for ya."

"You don't have to do that for us—" I started.

"But we'll be happy to oblige you—yes sir," Ollie finished.

"Alright, now git goin'. I'll be seein' youse all tonight," Handy said.

We continued down Main Street, passing the storefronts and townsfolk as if we were on parade. There were eighteen years behind us and a lifetime ahead of us. It felt final.

Our procession ended at the front door of the mercantile, where folks were hustling in and out, preparing for the weekend. In a town as small as St. Maries, everyone celebrated graduation, whether you had kin in the ceremony or not. Alumni returned to town filled with their successes; family and friends filed in from nearby communities and homesteads; churches and community groups hosted picnics and barbecues.

"Oliver, you get in here. Your mother and I have been looking for you," Mr. Hunt hollered from inside the store.

"I should have known better than to stop by here." Ollie skulked in through the door, made his way past the customers to the back of the store where his folks were waiting.

"What's he in trouble for?" Phoebe asked.

Drew and I looked at each other. "It could be darn near anything," I said. "Ollie's always spouting off. Most likely something he said just caught up with him."

We walked the length of the front porch for a few minutes, trying not to act curious about Ollie's fate. Several times we glanced through the window, but couldn't see Ollie through all of the customers. Suddenly Mr. Hunt appeared in the doorway. "The rest of you, get in here."

We looked at one another and then complied. As we entered the store, we saw Ollie with his back to us, perched on a stool at the counter. There were five more stools placed next to him. Mr. Hunt's Bible was open in front of Ollie.

"Take a place up at the counter. I'll be right back."

He motioned us toward the stools and then disappeared through the kitchen door. Ollie didn't look up as we each took our seat. He was noticeably embarrassed that our afternoon was going to be interrupted by his father's preaching. Mrs. Hunt stood behind the counter, watching the customers behind us. We waited.

After what seemed an eternity, Mr. Hunt emerged, flanked by Ollie's brother and two sisters. Their heads were hung, undoubtedly because they were looking forward to a Friday afternoon church ceremony about as much as we were. Even Phoebe looked bothered by the interruption.

"Thank you for joining us here this wonderful afternoon as we celebrate the goodness of God," Mr. Hunt started. Ollie squirmed. I started thinking about our trip. Drew was on his best behavior. Both he and Anna listened politely, as did Phoebe. Isabel leaned on both elbows, staring right through Mr. Hunt to the wall behind. Mrs. Hunt didn't move from her post.

"I'm not sure I'll ever get this chance again, as tonight represents the start of your life's journey," said Mr. Hunt. "From now on, your trail isn't blazed and your route isn't mapped out. No one can give you advice to keep you on task and the wisdom that comes from experience isn't yours yet. Your parents can no longer absorb life's set-backs for you—in short, you're on your own." Mr. Hunt brushed a hand over his moist eye, which got everyone's attention, even Ollie's. "Mrs. Hunt and I hold each of you dear. You have filled our store with laughter and treated us with respect. For that we're grateful." Mrs. Hunt came forward and stood beside him. She reached over and caressed Isabel's face and then Phoebe's.

"I'm amazed at how the two of you keep up with these boys—I mean men—and still remain so sweet. Even you, Isabel, behind your lures and fishing poles."

I wondered what this was leading to, even though it felt good to be reminded how much we were cared for and loved. I'm confident that each of us was wondering when Mr. Hunt was going to get to the Bible. We kept ourselves prepared for boredom. Mr. Hunt reached down and took his Bible in his callused hands.

"Within these pages lie answers and truths common to every man, relevant in all seasons, true in every statement, and waiting to be released by whoever dares. Live in the pages, breathe the knowledge they hold, and know the peace that comes from a life in obedience to them. Don't take my word or any other person's, but experience for yourself the relationship present in this text." He paused and then nodded to Mrs. Hunt, who placed a crate on the counter. "Oliver, Phoebe, Isabel, Jackson, Andrew . . . God be with each of you." With that he reached into the crate and pulled out a brand new, leather-bound Bible for each of us. Our names were elegantly imprinted on the covers and leather bookmarks were sandwiched between the pages. I opened mine and on the inside cover Mr. Hunt had written, "No one can serve two Masters. He will hate the one and love the other. Luke 16:13. Choose this day who you will serve, Jackson, for by not choosing, you have already chosen." I missed the rest of Mr. Hunt's speech, not fully understanding what the statement meant but knowing well enough it was something worth getting.

Eventually we dismounted our stools and made our way back to Main Street, each of us clutching our gift. We headed east toward the St. Maries Hotel and were approaching its front steps, when a loud voice came from Hap's Tavern, right next door. It was Batum.

"You sons-of-bitches, get your hands off me!" he yelled. "It's not like I killed the bastard, even though he deserved it." The sheriff had recruited Hap to get Batum under control. Even with cuffs on, he presented a problem.

"Listen, Schrag, you can't go knifing a guy because he calls you a horse thief, rightly or wrongly.

It's against the law, and it's the law I'm here to uphold."

Once out of the tavern, Batum quieted down.

"Thanks, Hap," the sheriff said. "He'll be under my watch for a spell and won't be bothering you. Get me a list of the damages and I'll make sure that he takes care of them. And get that guy over to the doctor. We don't want an infection to set in."

Hap straightened his apron and turned back toward his tavern. The sheriff wheeled Batum around, which placed us directly in his path. Batum's eyes met Drew's and then quickly shifted over to Anna. The sheriff, oblivious, let go of Batum's cuffs for a moment to adjust his gun belt. It was long enough for Batum to attack.

Drew let go of Anna's hand and pushed her behind, bracing himself for the impact. Batum lowered his head like a bull on the charge and speared Drew with a blow that sounded like a whole side of beef dropping from a butcher's hook. Drew retaliated, hooking Batum's head with his arms, relying on the advantage of Batum's handcuffs to give him an edge. Batum took a bite out of Drew's forearm.

The sheriff lunged after Batum and caught him around the waist. Ollie, who was next to Drew, jumped on his back. It was like a fox jumping on the back of a grizzly. Batum finally succumbed to the strength of three men. The sheriff pinned him to the ground with his boot between Batum's shoulder blades. Even when he was bound physically, Batum's mouth was unstoppable.

"You little shits. I'm gonna whip your asses, you hearin' me?"

"Doesn't seem like you're in any condition to make threats, Mr. Schrag," Ollie said. Drew elbowed him to shut up.

"Listen here, Hunt," said Batum. "When I get through with you, you'll be in no condition to even move."

The sheriff hoisted Batum up by his cuffs, this time gripping tightly as he escorted him. "And after I whip your ass, Featherweight, I'm gonna have my way with that whore next to you."

The sheriff shoved Batum ahead, and then they disappeared around the corner on their way to the jail house. Drew grabbed hold of Anna, who was shaking uncontrollably.

"He won't touch you, Anna. I swear it," Drew said through his teeth.

Chapter 14

Drew walked Anna home, and left only after the sheriff confirmed Batum would be locked up for at least 90 days. Following supper, we all met at the school and readied ourselves for the ceremony in one of the classrooms. The three men showed up in starched shirts. Isabel and Phoebe arrived a few minutes later, each wearing a dress.

"Oliver Hunt, if you say one word about this dress, I'll box your ears," Isabel said.

"What do you take me for, some sort of cad?"

"Actually there are more descriptive terms I might use."

"Once again, I'm hurt. . ."

"Ah, hell, I'm gonna give you a good wallop just because I know what you're thinking."

With that, Isabel popped Ollie up alongside the head. Ollie grinned.

"That's what I thought," she said, turning away.

Ollie didn't even retaliate; the spirit of the evening had given him some new sense of tolerance. There was a knock at the classroom door. I opened it and there stood Mrs. Sorensen.

"May I come in?" she asked.

"It would be our pleasure," Ollie shouted from the back of the room. He received a glare from Phoebe for his enthusiasm.

"I wanted to stop by and wish each of you good luck. You're a bright group, a joy to teach over the past four years. I'll miss you all." Miss Sorensen straightened her dress. "Well, people are already starting to gather. This is your moment."

"Thank you, Miss Sorensen. You've been a real inspiration," said Phoebe. She reached into the bag that had carried her cap and gown and pulled out a nicely wrapped box. "This is a little something from all of us." Phoebe eyed Drew, Ollie and me, letting us know that one word to show we had no idea what was going on would be entirely inappropriate. Miss Sorensen smiled and sat down at one of the student desks to open her gift. It was strange to see her at a desk—a startling contrast to the authoritative figure we were familiar with. Miss Sorensen undid the wrapping as if she was defusing a bomb—each movement was carefully considered and accurately executed, in keeping with how she did everything else in life. Finally, out of the layers of tissue paper she produced a framed painting titled, "Miss Sorensen's Paradise." It was a portrait of St. Maries —the buildings along Main Street set against a backdrop of jutting mountains. There were townspeople on the sidewalks and everything seemed true to life except that all the men who would usually be wearing suspenders and caulked boots, they all wore a professor's robe and cap.

"Oh, class, this a precious gift indeed." She searched through her purse for a tissue. Taking the picture in both hands, she held it at arms' length in front of her. "This truly would be paradise. Thank you for something so special to remind me of you."

Drew, Ollie and I smiled vaguely, trying to affirm we'd known about the present all along. Miss Sorensen rose and gave Phoebe a hug. She did the same with each of us, including Ollie. As she approached him, he was licking his lips as if preparing for his first kiss. Instead of embracing him, Miss Sorensen reached out and shook Ollie's hand. "I'm sure your contribution was considerable, Oliver." Drew and I burst out laughing, while Isabel and Phoebe merely smirked. And there Oliver Hunt stood, his prowess in romance thwarted by an ordinary handshake.

The band had started warming up in the Assembly Hall. It took over a dozen measures of the song until the music became recognizable as "Pomp and Circumstance," and then only if you possessed an active imagination. Miss Sorensen left the five of us to endure our nerves until the ceremony began.

Finally, the knock on the door came, signaling it was time for us to move into the hallway. Standing up, I wobbled a little, but Drew came up behind me and steadied me.

"Jackson, can I talk to you for a minute?"

"Drew, this is a hell-of-a time for conversation—can it wait?" But, from the look on Drew's face, this was a conversation that would wait for no one. "Alright, what's it about?" I said. He grabbed me by the arm and tugged me to the opposite side of the room, away from our classmates.

"It's about those letters that we wrote the other day in class."

I waited for him to continue his thought. He didn't. "What about them, Drew? Are you afraid Miss Sorensen's going to publish yours in the Gazette?" I said with a laugh. Drew didn't join me.

"Would she?"

"Of course not."

"Read them or publish them?"

"Either!" Where this was going, I wasn't sure. But I did know that Ollie, Isabel and Phoebe were heading for the door. "Look, Drew, if you're regretting something that you wrote, there's not much you can do about it now. Besides, they're just stupid letters—who cares if she reads them or not?" I slipped on my gown and placed my cap carefully on top of my head. "Come on, Drew," I said. "We'll miss our entrance." I made my way across the room. Looking over my shoulder, I saw that Drew hadn't budged an inch. I nudged Ollie.

"I think he's got a bad case of nerves. Maybe he needs some encouragement."

"Andrew Featherweight, get your fat ass moving!"

Drew looked up at Ollie, but stayed still.

"What's bugging him, J.D.?"

"I'm not sure—something about that letter we wrote in class, the one that Miss Sorensen said she was going to keep."

"What the hell?"

"I don't know. Your guess is as good as mine."

"Drew, snap out of it," Ollie said walking toward him. Phoebe and Isabel stood motioning us to hurry. "Come on. We're expected in the Assembly Hall right now. Have you forgotten?" Ollie said.

"J.D. said she might print them in the Gazette."

"Print what in the Gazette?"

"The letters."

Ollie turned to me for clarification. "I was joking, Drew. Miss Sorensen's not going to open them."

"But what if she does?"

"What if she does, Drew?" Ollie retaliated.

"Just that my life as I know it is over, that's all." Drew's hands started to shake. "I wrote things I shouldn't have written—anywhere."

Isabel broke in. "We're going to march out there without you, just me and Phoebe. No one will miss you, anyhow."

"We're coming, just hold on," Ollie said. He put a hand on Drew's shoulder and said the kindest thing I'd ever heard out of his mouth. "Listen, Andrew. Whatever's bugging you, we'll settle, it, understand? There's nothing we wouldn't do."

Drew took a deep, shaky breath. "You mean that?"

Ollie and I both shook our heads yes. "Let's get out there and graduate," I said. "And before the night is over, we'll figure out what to do about the letter."

Finally, Drew put on his robe and the five of us followed each other into the Assembly Hall for the last time.

Chapter 15

The ceremony was short, as we had figured. Phoebe made a speech about the promise of the future and Miss Sorensen finished by telling us we were all destined for greatness. Her words were a stretch, to say the least. Probably a quarter of the men and women in the audience couldn't read, and many of the rest had no more than a sixth grade education. Once you landed in St. Maries, it was tough to escape. The faces of the audience told us: despite how assuredly we might think life was what we made of it, or that anything could be achieved if we set our minds to it, the truth was life was a struggle and there was much more of a possibility for failure than there was for success. The closer we came to leaving the safe arms of our youth, the more evident it became.

After the ceremony was over and our families had doled out hugs, kisses and congratulations, Ollie, Drew and I lingered in our chairs on the makeshift stage of peeled poles and rough-cut timbers. The spotlight had been removed, but we weren't through basking in its glow. People wandered around below us. Like any other ceremony, the purpose of the gathering quickly melted into a vague sense of community. Now that we'd gotten our diplomas, people used the time to catch up with each other and we were all but ignored.

"What time should we meet in the morning?" Drew asked, settling back in his chair.

"No sense getting too excited, I reckon. The barge doesn't leave until two o'clock," I replied.

"Come on, you two. I'll be up by first light and you know you will be, too." Ollie said.

"Why don't we meet at the mercantile at ten?" Drew and I nodded. He was right.

Handy's voice cut through the din of conversation as he approached from behind us on the other side of the stage. "Hail, I cain't believe they's let the three of youse hawn-yawks gradiate!" he said. We turned toward his voice, but were startled when it didn't match the person we expected. Standing before us was a clean-shaven man in a brown tweed suit, polished shoes, and slicked hair. The only familiar detail was the stump in place of his left hand.

"Handy?" we said simultaneously.

"Sure the hail is. Who'd youse expect, Rockefella?" I'd never seen Handy without a layer of soot and grease covering his face and he was surprisingly handsome.

"Where'd you get the duds, Handy?" I asked.

"T's ordered 'em from the Sears 'n Roebuck. Not bad fer a blacksmith, eh?"

"Not bad at all," I said. He posed for us, his right hand tucked in the pocket of his vest and his left arm hung by his side. I reckon he would have stood there all night if we hadn't offered him a chair.

"Does the offer still stand to bring by our horses in the morning, or was that a moment of weakness?" Ollie asked.

"Shiii—I's afraid you was gonna remember dat," he said, smiling. "I's be ready for you by ten o'clock. Any earlier 'n I reckon youse be out of luck."

"You plan on getting home a little late tonight, Handy?" Ollie said.

"Hail, with any luck, I won't make it home at all, boys." He jumped to his feet, did a little jig, and stepped off the stage. "Time to git out there 'n find the dollies! See youse hawn-yawks in the mornin'."

Anna, who'd been talking with Phoebe and Isabel, made her way to where we were sitting, her long hair and dress following like a bridal train.

"Where are your brothers, Anna?" Drew asked.

"We're staying in town tonight." She glanced nervously over at Ollie, then back at Drew. "Mrs. Hunt was kind enough to invite us to stay for a spell."

"A spell," Ollie blurted. "How long's that?"

"A spell is however long I say it is, Oliver Hunt." Ollie's mom said, stepping in. "Besides, you won't need your room for a while. You'll be spending nights on the hard forest floor. For the meantime, Anna will be in your room and her brothers in the guest room."

"Wait a second," Ollie said. "Where am I gonna sleep tonight?"

Mrs. Hunt put her arm around her son. "One night on the sofa won't hurt. In fact, it might help break you in for the nights ahead."

Ollie let out a chuckle. "You just want me on the sofa so I can keep an eye on the front door and make sure Drew doesn't do any midnight calling." Mrs. Hunt and Drew both gave him a healthy whack while Anna blushed.

"Take it easy on that cute little man." Ollie wheeled around just in time to meet Boathouse Nellie's embrace. "There's no way I'm gonna let an opportunity like tonight go by without giving the three of you a squeeze," she said. Nellie buried Ollie in her chest, and kissed the top of his head. She released him, which sent him back on his heels, struggling to regain his balance. Nellie continued down the line, giving Drew a bear hug and a peck on the cheek since he was so big, and ending with me. By this time, Ollie had regained his composure and noticed his mother, whose eyes were as big as her mouth, having seen her son in the arms of the town whore.

"Oh, mom, let me—uh, let us introduce you to—um, well I reckon you know Boathouse—"

"Miss Nellie, it's good to see you," Mrs. Hunt interrupted. "I wasn't aware that you'd made my son's acquaintance."

Nellie smiled. "Oh, didn't they tell you? Why, it was the highlight of my week when they came calling a few days back." Mrs. Hunt raised an eyebrow at Ollie and Anna stared at Drew, who were both white as ghosts, undoubtedly just shy of fainting completely. The attention directed away from me was a relief, but still I found myself wringing my hands so hard I could feel it in my bones. "As a matter of fact, this one is the youngest man that has ever graced the covers of my bed," she said as she pinched my stomach.

It was obvious Nellie understood the dynamics of the situation, but had decided to have a little fun at our expense. I think she would have continued if not for Phoebe saving all of us, as usual.

"Nellie, it's good to see you. How's your cold?"

"Much better, sweetie, thanks to you and these fine young men."

Mrs. Hunt and Anna turned toward Phoebe disbelieving and confused.

"You were in on this, Phoebe?" Mrs. Hunt asked. Realizing the implication, Phoebe blushed.

"Oh dear," was all she could get out.

Nellie giggled. "I think you kids have some explainin' to do to poor Mrs. Hunt and this little sweetheart," she said.

Phoebe cleared her throat, fidgeted with her dress, and looked up at Mrs. Hunt, whose expression was chilling.

"Mrs. Hunt, surely you don't think—"

"I'm not sure what to think, but I do know what I don't want to think, so you better not be thinking what I am, or each of you is going to be thunked!"

Anna nodded, agreeing silently with Mrs. Hunt's brief tirade. Nellie stopped giggling, and reached over to take Mrs. Hunt's and Anna's hands, as Phoebe was completely flustered and the three of us men weren't about to venture into the midst of this one.

"Phoebe was kind enough to do my laundry last weekend, when I had a cold that was just short of death itself. She enlisted the help of these fine young men, who were kind enough to drink some of my lemonade and keep me company while Phoebe hung the garments out to dry. It was one of the most enjoyable afternoons I've had in a long time, Mrs. Hunt. They were perfect gentlemen."

Anna and Mrs. Hunt appeared to be satisfied by Nellie's explanation. Drew and Ollie regained their color and Phoebe let out a sigh of relief.

"Well, I have pies fresh from the oven over at the house – let's all meet there before going over to the hotel. Miss Nellie, won't you join us?"

"Do join us," Phoebe encouraged.

"Oh, I don't know—" Her eyes dropped. "It's one thing to be seen in public, but in your own home—"

Mr. Hunt, who had joined the crowd, interrupted. "But our own home is where the rest of us sinners gather, Nellie. If you'll overlook our faults, we'll oblige you the same."

Nellie smiled, silent with emotion. Mrs. Hunt and Phoebe linked arms with Nellie, leading her out of the Assembly hall, with Anna walking beside. The four men fell into step and we all walked into the night onto Main Street, together.

We ended up meeting Mr. Miller and Isabel as we crossed over to the mercantile. Handy took a break from his quest for female attention to indulge in the feast Mrs. Hunt had put together, and my folks, along with the parents of my other classmates, all joined us at the Hunt residence. Mr. Miller had brought two tubs of ice cream to go with Mrs. Hunt's pies, and Mr. Hunt had Drew and me pull a couple of cases of root beer and sarsaparilla from the cooler.

By the time it was all gone, no one had a spare square inch left.

"I'll commit the adults here to clean-up the table and help with the dishes," Mrs. Hunt said. "You kids have the night off."

Drew, Ollie, and I knew not to question or comment, but simply fold our napkins and push ourselves from the table.

"Great! Looks like everything's covered," Ollie said. "Drew forgot his bag at the school, so we're going to stop by there before we meet you at the hotel." With that, we were out the door before our consciences could catch up. Once we were outside, Ollie dashed to the back door of the mercantile, disappeared through the door and reappeared carrying an envelope and a pad of paper.

"If we're going to steal the one, we have to replace it with another," Ollie said. We made our way down Main Street. I noticed Drew was hanging back.

"Don't tell me you're having second thoughts?" Ollie asked, still striding forward.

Drew shrugged. Ollie slowed so he could catch up. "I mean, maybe she won't even open them."

Ollie stopped both of them. "Listen, as far as I'm concerned, it's the best excuse we have to do something stupid on graduation night."

"So if she never opens anyone's envelope, you two won't be sore at me?"

Ollie didn't miss a beat. "Only if we get caught, and then I plan on blaming it all on you, anyway."

Drew cuffed him. "Well hell then, let's do it."

By the time we arrived at the school, everything had been shut down. The lights were out in the main building and the chimney had only a trickle of smoke, as the fire in the furnace was all but dead. As we made our way around to the west side of the building, we could see a lone light on in the Assembly Hall.

"Must be Mr. Frankle," Ollie whispered.

As we got closer we saw that it was indeed Mr. Frankle, sweeping the Assembly Hall floor. Mr. Frankle was a German immigrant who lived in the boiler room during the winter and in the garden shed during the warmer months, taking care of the building and surrounding grounds. He was never called by any title, probably because that made it easier to justify his meager salary.

Since Miss Sorensen's room was in the main building, Mr. Frankle's presence was a minimal threat. Not to mention he was hard of hearing and could only see out of one eye. Ollie vanished to the east side of the building while Drew and I tried each of the exterior doors without any luck. Just as Drew shook the last of the doors, we looked up and there was Ollie's face pressed against the inside of the glass. I let out a yelp and Drew jerked back, letting go of the doors and losing his balance. I tried to catch him but he toppled down. Ollie popped the door open.

"Did I forget to tell you that I left a window open when we were getting our gowns on?" he said, smirking.

Drew dusted off his shirt and followed me through the door Ollie held open. We made our way down the hall without any light, led only by familiarity. Once inside Mrs. Sorenson's room, Ollie closed the door behind us, pulled a candle from his pocket, and lit it with a match. Its glow cast distorted shadows on the surrounding walls.

"Kind of spooky, huh?" Ollie said. "Just think, up on the Joe, it'll be darker than this. The only thing that'll light the night are the good Lord's stars." He paused for a moment, and then continued, "No telling what'll be lurking in the shadows, then."

The whites of Drew's eyes reflected what little light there was. "What do you mean?" he said.

Here it came. Drew had taken the bait and was effortlessly reeled in. "Didn't I ever tell you about the footprints I saw on my last trip to Boulder Creek?" Ollie raised the candle, its light glistening off of the beads of sweat on Drew's forehead. A warm breeze blew in from the window Ollie had left open. "Yes sir, footprints that would make yours look like a ballerina's, Andrew Featherweight. And they weren't human, neither."

"Ollie, maybe you shouldn't—"

"That's exactly what I thought, Jackson, exactly what I thought. Maybe I shouldn't tell the Forest Ranger what I found, except that it was the Forest Ranger *who* I found. Chewed up like a mound of hamburger, right where the footprints ended." Drew's eyes were wide open, unblinking. "Then, just beyond where the Forest Ranger lay, I heard a noise—" As if on cue, the wind rustled some papers hanging on a wall nearby. "A shadow appeared from behind a tree, and then..." Ollie raised the candle just below his chin, "...came..." Ollie grabbed Drew's shoulder and yelled, "...the beast!" Drew swung his arms out as if readying himself for an assault, toppling over an oak filing cabinet behind him. It crashed to the ground, the drawers flew open, and their contents spilled. When everything had settled, the three of us were poised ankle deep in a pile of papers and folders that Miss Sorensen had meticulously filed away.

Attempting to gain control of the situation, Ollie lowered the candle to the ground. "Well," he said, "this is as good a place to start looking for those letters as any." He started to shuffle through the mess, lifting each folder and rifling through its contents, then piling it to the side. Drew and I pulled the drawers the rest of the way out and set the cabinet upright. We joined Ollie in looking for the letters.

"Bingo!" Ollie held up a stack of envelopes with a string tied around them. He quickly untied the bundle and shuffled through until he found Drew's letter.

"Here it is, my friend."

Drew snatched the envelope out of Ollie's hand. Ollie handed him the pad and pencil he'd gotten from the mercantile, and Drew started writing another letter. He tucked the original in his jacket pocket.

"Now that it's in hand, how about telling us what's so important about that letter?" I asked.

"No offense, J.D., but I'm not sure I want you to know," he muttered, continuing to write.

Ollie grabbed the metal wastebasket at the side of Miss Sorensen's desk and turned it upside down, dumping its contents. "Well, then, give it here and I'll burn it."

Drew paused for a moment from his writing. "Quit pushing me, Ollie. The envelope will stay with me." That ended our discussion.

"What do you suppose on doing with this mess?" I asked Ollie, since Drew was preoccupied with his letter.

"Wait here—I'll be right back."

With that, he vanished into the black hallway. I heard the back door shut behind him. Moments later, he reappeared with Phoebe in tow.

"What the hell?" Drew said.

"Phoebe did most of Miss Sorensen's filing. She said she can have these cabinets back in shape in no time," Ollie said.

"Did you cart Anna and Isabel over too?" I asked, half joking.

"I told them you and Drew would be over in a few minutes. Phoebe and I can take care of the filing."

"It's alright, Andrew. Oliver told me about your letter. I think it's sweet," Phoebe said.

Drew screwed up his face. "Ollie doesn't even know about the letter. How the hell could he have told you about it?"

Phoebe craned her neck in Ollie's direction. "Excuse me?"

"I think Drew has some explaining to do," Ollie said. "Obviously he has us all confused. We risk our reputations and honor and he doesn't even have the decency to let us in on the details."

Drew put down his half-finished letter. "I guess I do owe you an explanation—I'm just a little nervous, that's all." He reached in to his pocket and pulled out the envelope. "The truth is I wrote some things in this note that could get me in big trouble."

"That much we know—tell us something we don't," Ollie said.

Drew looked around at our faces dimly lit by the one candle. "In this letter, I admitted to a crime I'd carry out if I had the chance."

The breeze suddenly stopped and the air hung heavy in the room. The only sound was constant breath of those in the room.

Chapter 16

That evening at the St. Maries Hotel was splendid. Everyone from the ceremony was there, along with the rest of the townspeople and their kin. The Spokane and the Georgie Oaks were docked behind the hotel, serving as floating dance floors for the overflow from the hotel. And despite our protruding stomachs, Drew and I managed to take in our share of the delicacies.

The beauty of the evening went beyond the decorations on the walls, the gowns and suits, and the majesty of the ornate St. Maries Hotel. Truly beautiful were the men dancing with their wives and daughters; brothers, sisters, cousins, aunts and uncles coming together from all parts of the town and county; young romance being kindled; and a night that was clearer and brighter than any one I'd seen. Stars sparkled as the cool, dry air swirled up toward the heavens. Drew and Anna danced throughout the night, Anna compensating for Drew—it looked like a bull moose dancing with a gray fox, the one clumsy but determined, the other graceful and elegant. Romance was in the air for those fortunate enough to catch it—even our own Isabel Wainwright was pursued by the Schilling boy, Jacob. Turned out he was heading back to his lookout above Avery the same time we were. Can't say I blame him, seeing as it'd be months before he'd see another human being, let alone one in a dress.

Drew and Anna were giving their feet a break, so I made my way over to them. "I reckon Ollie and Phoebe should have been done by now," Drew whispered. I could barely hear him over the band. "Maybe you should go over and check on them."

"If I know Ollie, he'd have my nougats if I was to show up there unannounced," I whispered back. "I'm going over to talk with Jacob to see if I can get any last minute insights. I'll see the two of you later."

Drew and Anna smiled courteously, and then went back to gazing at one another incessantly. He would make eye contact and she would glance down at the floor, then he would lean over to make a comment, which she would respond to briefly. As if on cue, they would turn away from one another and after an uncomfortable moment, start the cycle over again.

Isabel and Jacob were sitting at a table in the corner of the lobby, away from the noise and mayhem. Although they, too, were obviously becoming enamored with each other, it was a totally different approach than Drew and Anna's. Isabel had her dress hiked up above her knees, cooling off from their turn on the dance floor, and her feet propped on a nearby chair. Jacob reclined in a seat across the table from her and they were laughing and shouting back and forth.

"Hello there, Isabel," I said.

"Hey, J.D. Take a load off and join us."

"Reckon I will."

"J.D., this is Jacob. He's the son of Mr. and Mrs. Schilling." Isabel turned toward me. "This here is Jackson Donner, one of my former class mates."

Jacob extended a hand. "Good meeting you, Jackson. Heard you're heading up my way for a stint," he said, settling back.

"How'd you know?" I asked.

"I was in at the mercantile getting the last of my supplies when Mrs. Hunt mentioned her son and two of his friends were heading up there after graduation."

"That's us, alright," I said. "How many horses will you be packing in with?"

"Not a one. I'm taking the first run of the new railroad between here and Avery. Leaves at dawn tomorrow. I reckon if the three of you had any inclination to join me, I could arrange a ride for you and your horses. It'd cut a good week off your journey."

My heart skipped. It's not that I wasn't excited about the adventure ahead of us, but the thought of reaching our destination in hours rather than days, well, let's just say the appeal was there.

"In fact, you're welcome to set up camp at the ranger station in Avery. We have bunks and on a good day, even showers."

The temptation was growing. "I'll talk to—" I stopped. What was I thinking? There was no way Ollie would consider doing anything less than what we planned. In fact, it was for just that reason—the intrusion of the railroad – that first inspired Ollie to make the trip. In truth, it had been a primary motivator for me as well. "Ah heck, I appreciate the offer, Jacob, but we'll stick to the trails."

"Suit yourself. I'm not due on the lookout until July, so I'll have a good meal waiting for you at Avery when you arrive."

"That sounds good. It'll give me something to look forward to."

I left the two of them to resume their conversation and walked into the night air, breathing in as much of St. Maries as I could. My thoughts began to roam and ended up with the injustice of being alone while my peers fell for each other, thinking about responsibilities I wasn't ready for. Fear and self-pity loomed against a backdrop of uncertainty. It seemed somehow that the world had just gotten cruel.

Chapter 17

I was up with the dawn as Ollie predicted; the morning clear and dry like countless before. The little amount of dampness that did exist was sure to disappear once the sun rose. My pack, sitting beside my bed, was just as I'd left it three nights ago when I had gotten it ready: my newly washed clothes folded neatly in the main compartment; an extra pair of boots tied on the side; and my bedroll and tarp rolled tightly across the top, their ends drooping over the sides. I pulled on my trousers and a shirt, fastened my suspenders, tossed the covers over my bed, and made my way down stairs. Being that it was Saturday, I was the first one in our house to get up. I started a fire in the stove and banged around a few pans, hoping the noise would prompt my Ma to take pity and cook me breakfast. It worked as planned.

"I hear you out there, Jackson, so you can quit the routine," she hollered from the room she and Pa shared. "Put the skillet on the stove to heat and I'll be right out."

I reckon on any other Saturday I would have felt bad about waking her so early, but that day was different. With graduation the night before and the three of us leaving in a matter of hours, I guess I just wanted a little attention.

"What'll it be, young man? Hominy and bacon or fried potatoes and sausage?"

"What about pancakes? Are they part of the deal, too?"

Ma scowled. "I suppose," she said.

Pa joined us, smelling the bacon and coffee. Then Pa and I got the last of my supplies together. We headed out the door with two packs, one carrying my goods and the other carrying the supplies.

"Sure is a hell of a long way to Avery, Jackson. Wouldn't you rather take a riverboat to Coeur d' Alene for a week and live it up on the lake?"

I placed the last of the utensils in the supply pack. "Pa, haven't you ever been so scared about something that you knew you just had to do it?"

He nodded. "Yep, guess I have."

"If it weren't for Ollie, I reckon Coeur d' Alene would be an option. Then again if it weren't for Ollie, I wouldn't have considered going in the first place." We loaded both packs on the back of the wagon. "We talked about it all through our school years—but now that it's nigh time to leave, I'm downright terrified. I've never been past Falls Creek where you built that splash dam a few summers ago."

Pa hitched up the team, keeping his concerns to himself. He never was one to give advice, even though there were times I felt I needed some. Instead, he would simply nod and say, "You'll get by." Maybe that's what I needed, but it sure as hell wasn't what I wanted. He reached under the buckboard of the wagon and pulled out a burlap bundle, then unraveled the worn rope around it and laid open several layers of cloth.

"Haven't gone into the woods without it, Jackson. Don't suppose you ought to, either." In his hand was a well-polished Remington revolver. "Man or beast, anywhere above St. Joe City, it's just you against them, that's it. No law, no neighbors, no kin. The chamber is full—I'm hoping it'll come back that way, but if you need it, Jackson, don't hesitate. Chances are whatever's on the other end won't wait for you to make up your mind."

Pa wrapped the revolver back up, placed it with the utensils, and laced up the pack. He untied the reins from the porch railing and swung up on the seat of the wagon. "Go say good-bye to your Ma, Jackson. She's in there about ready to get her boots on and go with you boys. She don't think you'll last two nights without her help." He smiled and motioned me inside.

Ma gave me a towel full of biscuits and cheese, a half-dozen strands of jerked beef, and two silver dollars. "You be safe, Jackson. That country up there can be mean."

"I can handle myself, Ma."

She fought back a tear in the corner of her eye. "I know you can, son. Whatever you do, you three stick together." She gave me a long hug, which felt good. Her embrace was confident.

"Send word by rail as soon as you make it to Avery." I gathered the food and dropped the silver dollars in my trouser pocket. Ma gave me a swat out the door. She stood on the porch as Pa and I headed to town. I looked over my shoulder as we crested the hill and she was still there, waving her hand until we disappeared out of sight. I turned back and faced the road ahead, hands trembling. The journey of my life was upon me.

Ollie was waiting when Pa and I pulled up to the front porch of the mercantile. We unloaded the two packs and Mr. Hunt came out to greet us. He and Pa talked while Ollie and I went to work loading the horses.

"Did you get those beasts shoed like I told you, Oliver?" Mr. Hunt asked.

"Handy's going to do that on our way out of town."

"Wouldn't want them without protection if they're to maneuver those rocky riverbanks."

"No sir," Ollie replied.

Pa and Mr. Hunt went inside, leaving us to our work. I cinched the supply pack, along with Ollie's food pack, onto the pack horse, leaving just enough room for Drew's goods. Then we waited. By eleven o'clock, Ollie was beside himself. He had sat an entire half-hour with nothing to do.

"Where in the hell is that big oaf?" he muttered, kicking the dirt and rock that made up Main Street. His tirade accomplished nothing. We continued to wait, speculating about how far we'd make it before sunset.

"At this rate, we'll be lucky to make it to the loading dock," Ollie said.

The next hour seemed like a lifetime to Ollie, and he finally declared he had waited long enough. We took the horses to Handy's, telling Mrs. Hunt to send Drew over when he arrived. Handy performed his one-handed miracles while he gave us an earful about his escapades the night before. As always, Handy had stories about his conquests. We politely cut him short. Ollie's patience was wearing thin, and there was still no sign of Drew.

"If that good-for-nothin' isn't waiting on the front porch of the mercantile when we get back, we're going to leave without him," Ollie said dragging the horses along Main Street. "It's quarter past one o'clock and that supply barge isn't going to wait for our sorry asses."

"We can always ride the train. Jacob said that they could probably make room for our horses—" Ollie stopped cold and spun on his heel.

"On the other hand," I said, "let's just hope Drew's waiting."

When we arrived, Drew's packs were sprawled out on the porch. I figured that would quench Ollie's fire; instead, it fueled it. He burst through the front door looking for Drew. I followed to run interference.

"How'd the shoeing go?" Mr. Hunt asked.

Ollie blew past his father and mine who were both standing at the counter. He barged through the kitchen door. Ollie was ready to attack, his face red and knuckles white.

"There you are, Oliver. You and Jackson sit down and join us in a glass of lemonade," Mrs. Hunt said. Drew, Anna, Phoebe and Mrs. Hunt were sitting at the table. One sight of Phoebe and Ollie's blaze cooled to campfire embers. We took a seat and Ollie regained his composure.

"Are those horses finally shoed, Ollie?" Drew quipped.

With Phoebe at his side, Ollie simply nodded his head. Drew continued. "Just been sitting here with these lovely ladies, hoping you'd hurry up. We have a boat to catch, or had you forgotten?" Ollie shook his head, displaying the poker face of a seasoned gambler. Drew gave up.

Mr. Hunt and Pa came in after a few minutes. Mr. Hunt, who was standing at the door so he could keep an eye on customers, was grinning.

"What's that look for?" Mrs. Hunt asked.

"Oh, nothing, I guess. Just been awhile since I've seen two such homely boys with two beautiful women...that's all." He and Pa cackled, while Mrs. Hunt swatted the air as if to reprimand them both. All of a sudden I wanted the trip to start immediately so that I could have my friends back and enjoy them unchallenged by the female competition.

"We better get going, huh?" After the question came out of my mouth, I realized it sounded abrupt.

"I guess it's that time," answered Mr. Hunt.

Mrs. Hunt herded everyone out the back door where she had a camera set up to take a photo. She took two shots of just the three boys, then finished with a couple group shots. As we were about to move from our places, Mrs. Hunt grabbed Ollie and Phoebe.

"It's not everyday I can find a young lady willing to stand next to my oldest and orneriest son for any length of time. I reckon that I want to get a record of it. No telling how long it'll be before it happens again." We all laughed except Mrs. Hunt, who was quiet and uncomfortably serious. Ollie and Phoebe obliged. Ollie cautiously slipped his hand around Phoebe's waist. Phoebe flinched but quickly relaxed. Ollie remained stiff as sun-dried leather, unquestionably petrified that he had gotten away with the gesture and uncertain what to do next. Nonetheless, Mrs. Hunt took the picture, which finally secured us passage into the wilds of the North Idaho wilderness.

After loading Drew's pack and goods on the horses, Pa and I pulled our wagon away from the mercantile, heading down to the docks. Following close behind were Mr. and Mrs. Hunt in their four seater, with Ollie and Phoebe snuggled in back. The horses were tethered to the back of the wagon, loaded down with our supplies and equipment. Drew and Anna decided to walk, since it was only a quarter of a mile to the loading docks. The boat wasn't scheduled to leave for another thirty minutes.

Just as predicted, the sun was already high and hot. Dust billowed as we drove the familiar stretch down Main Street. Traffic was surprisingly light, due in part to the festivities of the night before. We passed Mr. Miller who was busy washing his shop window.

"Today's the day, is it?" he shouted.

Ollie poked his head out from under the wagon's top. "Yes sir."

Drew, who was walking on the opposite side of the street, stopped for a moment. "Lost Lake and the tallest Tamarack," he said. "It's as good as done."

Mr. Miller paused and saluted. "Thanks, Andrew."

Drew waved back, took Anna's hand and followed the wagons to the dock.

Mr. Miller yelled after us, "I'll have cold sodas waiting," and in a voice barely audible over the sound of the wagons, "...so please return."

The next block, Handy was in front of his blacksmith's shop shoeing another mule. "Sons-a-bit'! I swear I ne'r had a whore giv'd me so much trouble as this ass."

"Good morning, Handy." Mrs. Hunt said as they passed.

"Ma'am, I ne'er seen ya. Do part'n my words, if ya please."

"Good day, Handy," she replied.

Handy tipped his soot covered hat and gave us a wink. "'Member to be sleepin' wit one eye open, boys. No tellin' what's be in them woods, ya hear?"

We continued past the St. Maries Hotel, which was still recovering from the night before. Streamers hung limp, having been partially torn down; a hand painted sign that once read "Congratulations" had all but fallen and was torn to merely "Congrat"; and the porch was littered with whiskey bottles, cigar and cigarette butts. Altogether these were the markings of a triumphant evening. We turned toward the river. I looked back over my shoulder and noticed the Hunts right on our tail, but lost Drew and Anna as we turned around the corner of the Hotel. Facing forward again, the river caught my eye, sun sparkling off its jade surface. Again, I was terrified. Not being distracted by the company of a young lady or involved in engaging conversation like my friends, I imagined what the river could hold in store. A surface so calm, but with depths so mysterious and stretches unknown. "I'll help Franklin unhitch the horses if you'll get the last of the supplies out of the back," Pa said when we arrived. My mind sprung back to attention.

"Where's Drew?" Ollie shouted. It turned out even Phoebe could only hold his attention for so long.

"He's just around the corner. Help me with these supplies and quit worrying," I said. "The supply barge hasn't even docked yet."

We readied the horses by strapping down the supplies on the sturdiest of the four, leaving the next strongest to carry Drew. Mrs. Hunt hollered occasionally from the wagon, where she and Phoebe were taking refuge from the sun. No sooner had we secured the loads than the whistle from the barge pierced the mid-day air.

"It'll be a few minutes while the barge refuels and takes on supplies. Doesn't look like it has a whole lot to unload, though, so you three best be getting ready," Mr. Hunt said.

"He's right," my dad said. "You boys better get those horses down next to the boat so they won't go off and leave you."

"We sure wouldn't want that to happen," Mr. Hunt said.

Between looking for Drew and keeping an eye on Phoebe, Ollie hadn't heard a word. I grabbed the reins, but the four horses were too much for me. "Oliver," Mr. Hunt said. "Help Jackson out. That boat's not likely to operate on your time schedule."

Ollie looked at his dad, dismayed, and then turned toward me.

"What?" his dad asked.

Ollie continued his trance, then gave his head a couple shakes. "Nothing dad, I'm fine," he said. He grabbed two sets of reins out of my hand and headed toward the barge. I followed.

"Something on your mind?" I asked.

"Don't know, Jackson. I guess I just realized beyond Falls Creek, we're on our own. I swear I could piss my pants right now and not feel a thing."

I wasn't sure what that meant, exactly, but I did know that if Ollie was scared, I was justified. We tethered the horses to a piling and located the captain of the barge.

"Avery?" he said. "Why the hell Avery? Ain't nothing worth doing up there. The only whore in town has the croup and is suspected to die by Sunday."

Ollie was at a loss for words. It seemed everything we were intent upon was losing its luster.

"I'll take you as far as St. Joe City. If the river weren't so low, I'd consider taking you to the Olson homestead, but rocks are showing in the deep pools, so I reckon St. Joe City's my limit." He spat a stream of tobacco on to the planks of the dock. "You lend me a hand navigating the river and unloading my supplies when we arrive and we'll call it an even deal all around. The whistle will signal our departure— don't be late."

Ollie dashed back up to the wagons without me. He went directly to the wagon where Phoebe and his mom were sitting, leaned his head into the wagon, and gave Phoebe his hand so that she could step out. Behind them, Drew and Anna came in to view, walking at a snail's pace. I realized then that, were it not for our inflated egos, the three of us would have elected to stay in the comfort of our known surroundings. However, bound by masculinity, we couldn't entertain any other options at this point.

Mrs. Hunt joined Pa and Mr. Hunt, and Drew and Anna came up alongside. Ollie hung back, holding Phoebe's hand. The whistle blew again. My heart raced and my vision blurred. Mrs. Hunt hugged me and I shook Mr. Hunt's hand. Pa ushered me toward the barge, as I struggled against my temptation to resist. When we had all reached the dock, Pa and I untied the horses, leading them on to the barge.

After securing the horses, I made final arrangements with the captain and went over my list which, by now, had been amended countless times. When I turned back toward the wagons I saw, silhouetted against the Main Street hill, Oliver Hunt and Phoebe Stockman kissing next to Andrew Featherweight and Anna Schrag who were doing the same. Mrs. Hunt tried not to notice while Pa and Mr. Hunt elbowed each other. I stared out of disbelief and envy.

The captain blew his whistle one last time and throttled the steam engine. He started untying his mooring ropes. "This is it, boys," he shouted. Ollie and Drew hustled to say goodbye to Pa and the Hunts. Mrs. Hunt was having the hardest time by far. I thought again of my Pa's advice to spend a week in Coeur d' Alene instead.

Drew and Ollie hopped on to the barge as it was pulling away from the dock. The three of us stood motionless, paralyzed by our decision. The waters churned, increasing the distance between us and our families and friends. The pilgrimage had begun.

Chapter 18

(North Idaho, Fall, 1979) "I always did want to cast a hook in this here lake, Lenny Dougherty." J.D. and Lenny had been driving for the past half-hour, while J.D.'s recollections were voiced.

"It's called, 'Turtle Lake.' See how the feeder stream at its east end makes a turtle's head?"

Lenny looked hard, employing all of his imagination. "Why haven't you?" he asked.

J.D.'s shoulders drooped. "Same reason I never hiked up to the top of Baldy, or jumped off the St. Maries River bridge, or tried fly fishing the headwaters of the St. Joe." J.D. turned his head toward the river, the hum of the highway and whine of the engine filling the silence between his words. "After our trip to Avery that summer, the call of adventure lost its appeal. Can't say it ever returned." He cracked his window to let fresh air circulate through the cab. "Can't say I ever wanted it to, either."

They continued to wind along the bank of the St. Joe. The river's current quickened the farther they traveled up river. The sun made its way across the mid-morning sky and the cool air warmed. The wind tossed around a few renegade clouds, but there looked to be no threat of rain. They continued to drive in silence.

Since Lenny didn't recall a city or any kind of settlement along this route, he reasoned that St. Joe City and J.D's friend's mill must be hidden on the south side of the river. Suddenly, J.D. pointed. "There it is!"

Lenny looked across the river but saw nothing. "Where?"

"Right there. Don't you see it?"

He slowed the truck and pulled off at a wide spot in the road. Lenny had a clear line of sight to the other side of the river, but still couldn't spot a single building. J.D. rolled down his window the rest of the way.

"Right there, Lenny Dougherty," he said as he pointed again.

Lenny peered into the woods lining the southern bank. Finally, hidden among the underbrush, remnants of a few buildings started to appear.

"That's St. Joe City?"

"What's left of her. The big mill used to sit about two hundred yards downriver from the rest of the town. You can still see the pilings. My friend's mill is another 25 miles or so upriver."

Sure enough, a few sets of logs were lashed together, most likely leftover pilings from the mill. They jutted out of the river's glassed surface.

"Is that where the barge you were on landed?"

"Yes sir, it is."

Now that Lenny knew what to look for, more buildings came into sight, beyond the overgrown trees and brush. He began to make out a main street lined with dilapidated storefronts just west of the bridge.

"When was it all abandoned?" Lenny asked.

"Abandoned? Hell, there are still people who live over there. The bridge flooded sometime back, but it's been rebuilt; other than that, St. Joe City still functions like it did at the turn of the century. There was a time when it thrived like any of the ports along the river. And even if all its businesses have shut down except the store, it still has its soul."

Lenny pulled back onto the highway and they continued upriver toward the St. Joe City turn-off. The buildings across the river continued to reveal themselves. A splintered sign was the only marker at the intersection. There, laid out in oil-soaked timbers, was a single-lane bridge that spanned the St. Joe River. Lenny sat idling for a moment.

"Go on," J.D. said. "It's good to cross.".

Lenny revved the engine and let out on the clutch. The truck lurched in response. The bridge creaked and groaned. His confidence continued to wane as they crossed and he found that the planks were deeply grooved by the countless other cars, making it difficult to maneuver. He fought to keep the front tires on track, but the bridge's ruts wouldn't let him keep control. The quarter-mile to the other side stretched out longer and longer.

"Just relax, Lenny. The bridge will do the driving for you." J.D.'s relaxed tone fueled his fear. "Let go the wheel," he said. "It'll take you—trust me."

Lenny looked over and J.D. winked at him. He slowly loosened his grip on the wheel, the color returning to his knuckles. With his hands loosened the truck followed the bridge precisely.

"Just like most things in life, Lenny Dougherty. Loosen your grip and see how things get easier," J.D. said.

When they reached the other side, Lenny steered them toward what had once been the thriving mill town of St. Joe City. J.D. pointed out landmarks as they idled down Main Street. As in any other small North Idaho town, people peered out of windows and from beneath hat brims at the unfamiliar truck and its passengers.

They left the east end of town, bumping over the unkempt road. J.D. directed Lenny toward what he remembered as the original mill site. As they approached, the mill's only visible remains made themselves evident – the pilings that interrupted the river's placid surface. J.D. took a deep breath.

"Pull over here, Lenny." He waved toward an abandoned road that led toward the river. They followed it to the river's edge and then J.D. motioned to shut the truck off. "We'll take it by foot from here," he said.

Before Lenny had even rolled up his window, J.D. was out of the cab, making his way down the overgrown road. Lenny followed close behind, striding to keep up.

"They'd haul the logs out of the water with a steam donkey, then skid them with a bull team to a landing lot over yonder. The wood sat there, waiting to be cut." J.D. pointed to each spot as he walked. "Customers cursed the mill for its high prices; the millwrights cursed the loggers and their sawyers for inconsistent lengths and quality; and the loggers cursed God for the toil it took getting the logs to the mill. A damned way of life, Lenny Dougherty."

Lenny nodded. He had learned about the hardships of the logging trade the little his grandfather had told him about his past. Aside from being away from home and family for weeks or months at a time, the environment itself was menacing. Sub-zero and near-starvation conditions during the winter took their toll and the possibility of being crushed by a falling crag was a constant threat.

But for those who survived the misfortunes of winter, the inescapable heat of summer and outbreaks of disease in the camps weren't far behind. With the advent of the rail system, accidents and catastrophes escalated. As J.D. had said, it was a rugged occupation for a hardened breed.

"On the cutting deck," J.D. continued, "the first set of saws trimmed each log into a square, workable shape. Then it would be cut into whatever the surveyor decided was most efficient for that particular log. If it was, say, an old-growth cedar, he'd choose a cutting sequence to get some good 2x12's or 4x12's for center beams, whereas if it was a jack pine, a trip to the stud line might be in order." J.D. continued as they came up alongside the river. Lenny's mind drifted. It was easy to see why they had chosen this site for a mill. There was a slow flowing bend in the river, which made a natural pool to float logs, and the bordering land sloped gently.

J.D. bent over and chose a flat rock from the countless supply on the river's edge. He cocked his arm and skipped it across the water. Lenny followed suit.

"Not bad for a city dweller," J.D. said.

"Just dumb luck," Lenny replied.

They skipped a few more and then stopped, staring together at the slow moving water.

"I wish I could do it all again, Lenny Dougherty."

"What's that?"

"Be on that supply barge, pulling up to the docks."

I chuckled. "You had that much fun with those two—what did Mr. Hunt call you—hawn yawks?"

J.D. spat into the water lapping at their feet. "Not for the enjoyment. To avoid what was waiting for us," he said, his voice tinged irritation. "Not one of us had any idea what we were getting into. God, why did we go?" With that, he turned back up the road to the truck. Lenny watched the pilings a moment longer, imagining the three of them stepping from the barge onto the first leg of their journey.

Back at the truck, the two climbed onto the worn seats. Lenny started the engine, then wheeled the truck back in the direction from which they'd come. J.D. returned to staring out the window in silence, apparently trying desperately to undo what could not be undone.

Chapter 19

Their second pass through St. Joe City yielded nothing but more looks from the locals. Lenny was looking forward to driving back across the bridge, this time with considerably less anxiety, when J.D stirred. "Pull over, Lenny," he said.

J.D. lurched out of the truck before it was completely stopped. He stumbled quickly, regained his balance, and made his way down to the river's edge, cautiously lowering himself next to the bridge abutment. Lenny stayed in the truck. After a moment caressing the bridge's base, J.D.'s hands stopped. He looked up, his eyes wide. Curiosity got the best of Lenny and he decided to join him; he had just shut the truck's door when J.D. let out a whoop.

"Here it is, Lenny Dougherty—right where we left it almost seventy years ago!"

Lenny crouched down next to J.D. All he could make out, though, was an old, rough, and abandoned concrete bridge abutment with a newer, sturdier one adjacent. "What has you so worked up?" Lenny asked.

J.D. continued to feel his way along the old pillar. It was laden with rock fragments, boulders from the river, and an occasional piece of metal. "The Forest Service built this bridge in the summer of 1910, to replace the wooden suspension bridge about a quarter mile upriver. They had just started excavating the day we arrived on the barge." He began chipping away pieces of the old concrete with a rock. "After the war and the advent of the automobile, they reinforced the bridge with the newer pillars. Never did tear down the originals."

A large chunk of concrete splashed into the river, revealing a small round cylinder of metal. J.D. dropped his chipping rock. He took his finger and wiped at the sand lodged around the metal. He beckoned Lenny toward him and it quickly became evident what J.D. had been looking at: there, staring them in the face, was the business end of a pistol.

"It's the one my daddy gave me when we left on our journey, Lenny Dougherty—the same one your granddad used to kill a man, three score and nine years ago."

J.D. let out a sigh. The words hung between them, a burden J.D. had apparently carried nearly all his adult life. Finally, J.D. had returned to the reason behind these stories. Both of them stared at the pistol. What was there to say next? Lenny reached out and touched the gun's metal barrel; the rest of the pistol remained buried in concrete abutment.

"I apologize for my method, young Lenny. To be honest, I wasn't sure how to tell you. I figure there's no good way with news like this."

Lenny nodded in silent agreement. It appeared his grandfather really had taken another man's life. Lenny knew he lived in a different time, but that he could have actually killed another human being, for any reason, was hard to comprehend. "Was it self defense?" Lenny asked.

J.D. tilted his head back, peering into the sky. "No, son, it wasn't." Lenny felt the blood drain from his head. He felt as though he was about to fall over. "I would call it an act of mercy, though I'm not sure the authorities would have agreed, had they ever found out."

Lenny stood there at the abutment, imagining an eighteen year old Andrew Featherweight firing that pistol at another person. His mind blurred.

Rocks tumbled and scattered as J.D. worked his way back up to the truck. He placed his hand on Lenny's as they got settled in the truck. "He was a good man, Lenny Dougherty. Forget the boards at my friend's mill—I'll get some at the hardware store later. Pilot us back to St. Maries and I'll explain the rest." As they started back across the St. Joe City Bridge, J.D. slid back into to the summer of 1910.

Chapter 20

(June, 1910) The barge ride upriver from St. Maries was uneventful. Any other year, the trip would have taken a good three hours but since the river was so low, the captain figured we'd hit the St. Joe City docks as early as four o'clock. Drew and Ollie were acting melancholy, their hearts apparently torn between romance and adventure. But eventually, important conversations distracted them: which one of us would catch the first fish, who cooked the best over an open fire, how skilled each of us were at lighting fires in the middle of rain storms. The closer we came to the rushing water of Falls Creek emptying into the river, the farther their heartsickness receded.

The docks of St. Joe City seemed to appear almost as quickly as the St. Maries had vanished. Just as the captain had predicted, we were unloading our horses and supplies after only a two-hour trip. We fulfilled our part of the bargain, helping him unload freight, and then ventured into St. Joe City, which turned out to be a great deal like St. Maries: makeshift buildings giving way to modern, well-built structures; townspeople more apt to be seen in jackets from the Sears & Roebuck catalog than their dungarees; and the balance between the number of churches and saloons heading towards even.

We stopped at the mercantile, which we decided wasn't as well-stocked or kept as the Hunts'. The shopkeeper was engaged in a hot debate with another local, about the advent of the railroad and its supposed impact on the local economy.

"Blasted!" he said. "It's sure to put me out of business. Why would anyone stop at St. Joe City when St. Maries is slated to be the rail hub? They already have the river boats, why should they get the railroad as well?"

"Sid, now settle down," his friend was saying. "It'll provide just the opposite. Everyone knows we have a better mill for floating logs. That'll help us maintain our edge over them sons-a-bitches to the west. You'll see what I mean—just wait."

"It's my guess that after the first fire their engines cause, the Union Pacific will be run out of Idaho, along with their promises of progress."

"God help us if anything causes a fire this year." With that they concluded their dispute, apparently satisfied by something they could agree upon.

We secured our supplies to our horses and started east out of town, along a trail beaten by loggers and forest rangers. Though it was well marked from frequent traffic, the trail was anything but convenient. In some places it was hard to believe that a supply wagon could maneuver the course.

Nonetheless, it was something to guide us and far more trustworthy than Ollie and his intuition. As we walked, the buzz of town faded, replaced by the tranquility of the forest. For the most part, the trail stayed about fifty feet above the river, occasionally dipping down a few feet from its shores. The farther east we went the faster the current ran and the water's color lightened, signaling the swift waters that were to come.

In the forested mountains of North Idaho, nightfall arrives long before it does in the open valleys and plains. Peaks and crags hide the retreating sun, with boughs of surrounding trees filtering out most of the remaining light. Dusk can sneak up and overtake you without warning. The customer at the St. Joe City mercantile had told us we'd reach the remains of a winter logging camp before night fall, so despite the fact that each of us had grown up in the woods, we ignored the warning signs. Because the sun waned gradually, our eyes grew accustomed to the depleted light. We got lost in our banter and it wasn't until I stopped to check my horse's hooves that I realized: I couldn't see a damn thing. I said it out loud and Drew and Ollie looked back. Peering around us, it became obvious that night had fallen.

We found a wide spot in the trail, tethered our horses and sat down in the dark for a meal of jerked beef and my mom's biscuits. We dared not light a fire, as the river was a good piece below and couldn't be reached quickly if it got out of hand. We were quiet in our disappointment. Other than Drew's horse stepping on his foot and Ollie narrowly avoiding a shower from his, the first night of our adventure was one to be forgotten.

Things improved after that first night as we became more familiar with our pace and routine. Breakfasts were piping hot coffee, crisp bacon, and fire roasted biscuits. Dinner meant freshly grilled trout and lunch happened whenever we had time— usually between fording the St. Joe and trying to land a fighting cut-throat trout on a nearby outcropping of rock. Then, more often than not, we would strip and cool ourselves in a fished-out pool, washing away the grime and grit of the afternoon.

It was early evening on the eighth day when we reached the fast water above Mica Creek, an area where the river creates a trough as it runs through the bordering meadows. A warm, dry wind poured through the valley, failing to bring any clouds to lessen the relentless heat. As we broke out of the woods and into one of the meadows, a homestead appeared on the opposite riverbank. Since they were folks not likely to get much company, we thought it might be decent of us to stop in. We made our way across the river.

Our welcome on the other side was not what we had expected. "One more step and I'll send you to meet your maker," came a husky woman's voice from behind a double barrel shotgun, aimed right at us.

Ollie was at the lead. "Ma'am, we were just passing by—"

"Well you can just keep passing, understand?" the woman said. Drew and I backed into the river, leaving Ollie to stare down the barrel.

"Why, yes ma'am, I suppose we could." Had he left it at that, we would have been on our way. But he didn't. "But after we've traveled so many miles, wouldn't it be hospitable to offer us something cool to drink?"

The gun's hammers clicked, positioned and ready.

A child appeared in the doorway of the cabin. My mind raced to the whereabouts of my daddy's gun, but my feet were anchored. Another child's face shone from the window of an outbuilding. And still another behind a wagon. They looked curious. The woman held her ground.

"Ma'am, this here is Andrew Featherweight," I started, "and I'm Jackson Donner, and the one you've got your sights on is Oliver Hunt. It's a pleasure to make your acquaintance." She shifted her body, but didn't lower the gun. "I reckon we surprised you, but we don't mean any trouble. We just graduated from St. Maries and we're headed to Avery for a spell of fishing and such." I couldn't believe I was speaking, but it seemed to work.

"Your kin own the mercantile in St. Maries?" she asked, peering over the gun's barrel at Ollie.

"Why, yes ma'am, they do. In fact, I've probably filled an order for you and your family if you stop by there."

She lowered the gun to waist level and slowly released the hammers, keeping it pointed at Ollie's mid section.

"I reckon you might of." Her eyes softened. "Now tell me again, what brings you to these parts?"

With that, she lowered the gun completely and we continued our conversation, making our way toward the house. It turned out Mr. and Mrs. Hunt had helped her and her husband get started when they moved to the St. Joe Valley from South Dakota, letting them barter for supplies. As we talked, the children wandered out of hiding: three of them, the oldest no more than ten. The youngest grabbed on to Drew's pant leg.

"Lissa, now you leave that man alone."

"That's alright, ma'am." Drew reached down and picked the little girl up.

"It's been two months since she's seen her daddy," the lady said, "so I reckon she's thinkin' you're him. He's about your size."

The two other children hung on their mother's dress, looking jealously at their sister and the attention she was receiving. I pulled two licorice sticks Mrs. Hunt had given us from my pack and handed them to the boy and older girl.

"Here's a something to keep you busy," I said. They glanced at their mother for permission, and then cautiously took the candy from my hand.

"What a treat! Sarah, Will Jr., what do you say?"

They mumbled a nearly audible 'thank you', already devouring the candy. The girl in Drew's arms looked more interested in basking in his strength than satisfying her sweet tooth.

"I should apologize for the way I greeted you," the woman said. "In fact, I don't think I've properly introduced myself. I'm Lillian Johanneson and these are our three children, Lissa, Sarah, and Will Jr." We shook hands with Will Jr., and patted the girls on the head. "With all the trouble in the past few days, I've been seeing more than my share of strangers passing. It's unnerving."

We nodded, but I wondered what kind of trouble she meant.

"How long the three of you been on the trail?" she asked.

"This is our eighth day, ma'am," Ollie said.

"Then you probably haven't heard. Six days ago a lookout spotted smoke just this side of the Montana border. Yesterday I got word they seen the fire headed our way. My husband Will was supposed to be home two days ago, but I got word the Forest Service is asking all logging and mining outfits to lend a hand. No telling how long he'll be gone."

Both Drew and Ollie were squinting upriver to see if there was any sign of smoke, but the only thing evident was warm wind blowing the meadow grass. Drew set the little girl down. She ran over and buried her face in her mother's dress.

Drew spoke: "Ma'am, we'd be much obliged if we could get a good night's rest and start out early in the morning. If the fire's bad enough to have the Forest Service spooked, I reckon they could use our help as well."

We set up camp on a flat spot just above the riverbank, tended our horses, then had a hot meal in the house. Ollie took Will Jr. down to the river after supper to test some flies he'd tied, as the evening calm settled over the St. Joe and trout surfaced for their evening meal. Drew and I watched from the front porch. We turned in just after nightfall, speaking little and quickly sinking into a sound sleep.

Chapter 21

We overslept the sun. The first one to wake, I worked to pry my eyes apart. It appeared a light fog had settled in the river valley. But after taking a deep breath, I discovered the haze was a layer of smoke. This realization jolted me up and into my clothes. No sooner was I out of the tent's entrance than my mind was relieved: pouring out of the chimney was the smoke from Mrs. Johanneson's cooking fire, trapped in the stagnant morning air of the valley. Relieved, I decided to get the most out of my momentary terror. I started whooping and hollering at Drew and Ollie.

"The fire's at our door!" I yelled. "Head for the river! It's our only chance!"

In a sleep-broken stupor, Drew and Ollie came scrambling out of the tent. I waved them past me, keeping up the appearance of frenzy. It wasn't until they were waist deep in the river that they realized I wasn't joining them. There, in the cold waters of the St. Joe, clothed in nothing more than their undershorts, Drew and Ollie swore like a couple of seasoned loggers.

"The cold water will get your heart started," I yelled from the safety of the riverbank.

They slogged back through the water. "I'm not so concerned about my heart as another organ that seems to have disappeared completely!" Ollie said as he scrambled up the bank.

Mrs. Johanneson called from the front porch, "Breakfast is ready when you are." She hesitated a moment when Drew and Ollie appeared over the bank. "A bit early for bathing, don't you reckon?" she called.

Drew and Ollie shook off the excess water as I followed Mrs. Johanneson into the house. I took my place at the table and Drew and Ollie appeared moments later in dry clothes. Lissa insisted she sit on Drew's lap.

"It's a good four days to Avery if you don't dawdle." Mrs. Johanneson filled our food sack with some fresh bread and a letter she'd written to her husband Will, in case we ran into him. "When you hit the mouth of Marble Creek, you have less than a day's journey to go. Cross the river just upstream and that will put you on the north side, the same side as Avery. God bless you each."

"Lissa, now let go of Andrew," Mrs. Johanneson said as she hugged each of us goodbye. She pried her daughter from Drew's arms. "He won't be any good to anyone with a little girl stuck to him like a tick."

Lissa whimpered. "She'll be alright," said Mrs. Johanneson.

Drew took off his hat and leaned down to kiss Lissa's cheek. He turned red as a tomato and hurried off the porch with Ollie and me close behind. Drew turned back. "One wise crack, Oliver Hunt, and you won't be chewing anything but your broken teeth for weeks." We struck camp, loaded our horses, and were on trail by half-past eight.

Conversation was sparse as we left the Johanneson homestead, our thoughts on the fire. We fished only for food, got in the water only when crossing the river, and rested just long enough to let the darkness pass over. Mealtime and trail talk were light, avoiding the topic. Even Ollie was solemn. Occasionally we'd get a waft of what we thought was smoke, but it was too faint to be certain since the air was so static. The steep hillsides of the St. Joe Valley kept us from seeing too far or knowing too much, a blessing as much as a curse. It wasn't until the fourth day since we'd left the Johanneson homestead, the twelfth day of our journey, that the demon first showed its face.

We crossed the St. Joe upriver of Marble Creek, just as Mrs. Johanneson had recommended. We worked our way up the north slope of the canyon with little effort—the trail was well worn and most of the underbrush had been cut back or was undernourished from lack of rain. Twigs broke, pine needles snapped and dust billowed as we continued to climb. The terrain leveled off about noon, when we broke into a clearing that gave us a vista of the valley below. The sight weakened my knees.

"God of mercy—" Ollie whispered.

No more than forty or fifty miles east, hundreds of square miles of green forest spewed forth white smoke. We could make out where the river wound its way through the inferno, buffering some areas from the fire's path but unable to safeguard others. To the north, the sheer rock cliffs of Lolo Pass forced the fire south and west; the hillsides of the southern valley reduced to charred scars. The fire had tipped over the mountain tops, into the adjacent valley beyond. Since there was no wind, the smoke trailed straight up and was starting to darken the sky. As we continued along the trail, we ate the last of Mrs. Johanneson's bread and a slice of smoked ham.   Then we pressed on to Avery, hoping to arrive by supper.

The trail continued paralleling the river below. Near four o'clock we began to descend into the valley, losing our ability to see the approaching fire. No sooner had we leveled off just above the river when the sounds of Avery broke through the silence of the woods and river.   Inside of thirty minutes we had tethered our horses outside of a local restaurant. Food was piled on each of our plates and Jacob Schilling, who greeted us just as we entered town, was telling us the details of the fire. Even as we spoke, the smell of smoke started to waft in.

"We sent a message by rail that we can use all the hands available. The word is that men are coming from as far west as Spokane, as far north as the Canadian border, east as the Dakota's, and south as Boise. By the time they get here, though, Avery could be in danger."

"In danger, hell, it'll be destroyed inside a week," came a bearded voice from a nearby table. "And if a westerly wind picks up, kiss your ass good-bye, boys." The man turned back to his table, tossed down the last of his drink and headed for the door.

"That's Edward Pulaski," Jacob said. "He's heading up the effort to the southwest, this side of the Marble Creek drainage. That's where we need help. You boys consider joining him?"

We nodded. "Alright, then. You can bed down in my bunk tonight; it's the sixth tent on your right. We'll start getting ready at first light."

Jacob rose from the table, paid our bill, and left us to finish our meal.

"You guys scared?" Drew whispered.

I glanced over at Ollie, who was putting bite after bite of food into his mouth until he could barely close it enough to chew.

Drew continued. "I mean, I never fought a forest fire before. Sure, I've seen my share of brush fires and such, but never a whole forest lit up. I don't know."

Ollie washed down part of his mouthful with a glass of water, then spoke before he'd swallowed the rest. "The way I see it, we don't have much of a choice. So it does no good to think about things that really don't matter." He spewed bits of food as he spoke, but the message got across all the same.

"I for one am a little concerned about waltzing off into an unknown territory to fight something as ruthless as a forest fire," I said. Ollie took his last bite and looked over at me.

"What am I stuck with, a couple of women?" Ollie said, well above a whisper. "I can't believe what I'm hearing. Maybe I'll go tell Jacob it'll just be me heading off tomorrow, because my traveling companions have decided to stay behind and peel potatoes."

Just as he was finishing a wide woman in a white apron came up behind him. She smacked Ollie on the back of the head. "And what, may I ask, is wrong with peeling potatoes?"

Ollie turned around and looked up. The woman easily dwarfed him. "You didn't let me finish, ma'am," he said. "I was going on to say I'd much rather peel spuds than fight some stupid fire, seeing as spud peeling is so much more noble an endeavor."

"Bullshiiit!" She gave Ollie another swat across the top of the head. "If there is anything I hate more than a mouthy, little boy, it's a lyin', mouthy, little boy. Now next time I hear anything like that, you best be lookin' for another wallop to knock some sense into you."

Drew and I smiled as she winked at us and gave Ollie another slap on the cheek. "So, you boys are in town to fight the fire, are ya?"

"Yes ma'am," I answered. "We started out to find a little adventure after our school graduation. Never thought it would end up like this."

"Hell, adventure is what you'll be gettin' once you set foot in those fiery woods. That you can be sure of. Finish up those meals—I've got some fresh cobbler to finish you off." She smiled, her teeth brown and yellow in the dim light of the Avery cookhouse, with greasy, matted hair outlining a plump, pock-marked face.

As she lumbered back to the kitchen, Ollie whispered, "That's Sister Louisa, I reckon. I heard about her from Handy. They say she's the only virgin in the St. Joe Valley and I can see why." We muffled our snickers for fear she'd hear us and deliver another punishment.

"Gooseberry cobbler for three brave boys. Eat up, 'cause it'll be the last good meal you'll be havin' for some time," she said.

On the front porch the sun had just started to dip out of sight behind the hills that followed the meandering path of the St. Joe River. Even in the short time we'd been in Avery the valley had begun to fill with smoke, drifting in the sun's rays.

With the impending threat, Avery was alive with activity. The mercantile, (if that's what you'd call it, since it was nothing more than a converted horse stable with crates of dry goods placed around) was busy loading wagons and pack teams with supplies for fire camps and lookouts; the saloons were loud and boisterous, already filled with tales of narrow escapes from death; the one church in town had a handful of do-gooders moving the church's organ for evacuation; and the blacksmith's shop was spewing black smoke into the night, as horses were shoed, axes sharpened, and tools poured. It was there we made our next stop; Edward Pulaski waved us over.

"I hear you're on my crew," he said.

"We're your ace in the hole, sir," Ollie said, stepping forward. Edward wasn't a big man. In fact, he was only a few inches taller than Ollie. His black beard was full and he had dark eyes to match. His curly black hair was tucked beneath a soft wool cap that looked like it hadn't been moved since the winter months.

"Where you boys from?" he asked.

"St. Maries. We just graduated and figured on coming up to Avery for a little adventure." Ollie said.

"Well, the adventure starts here, boys," his voice was calm but raspy. "Any one of you fought fire before?"

"Nothing more than a brush fire or someone's kitchen that got out of hand," I offered.

Edward tightened his lips. "Be at my tent at sundown and we'll go over some basics. The rest you'll have to learn as we go. By mid-morning tomorrow, we'll head out for camp and join up with the rest of the crew."

He hollered to the blacksmith that he'd be back at daybreak for the rest of his supplies, then left us standing in front of the shop, no doubt looking stupefied. A young boy, no more than ten years old, came out of the shop and approached us.

"You three fightin' the fire with Edward?" His eyes were wide.

"Looks that way, kid," Ollie replied.

The boy started to pace back and forth in front of us. "I told my Pa I'd go fight the fire, but he says he needs me to stay here and help out. I told him I was big enough to carry one of Edward's tools. See, I can handle it." He reached over for a tool that looked like the result of an ax and a hoe mating. He brought it above his head as if to chop a log, but its weight overcame him and toppled him backwards. Drew caught the tool and the boy before they both hit the ground.

The blacksmith came out of his shop. "Dammit, Ben! If I see you pick up that pulaski one more time, I'll wallop the seat of your pants with it!"

"Is that what you call it?" Ollie asked.

The man took the tool from the boy's hands. "Hell, I don't know whether that's what it's called or not, but it suits me, seein' that Edward's the one who designed it. I'll be up all night pouring casts to fill the demand. Every firefighter wants one."

The man set the pulaski down, then took the boy back inside the shop. Drew picked it up and wielded it as if he was chopping a log. "It has good balance," he said. Ollie took it from Drew to try. His motions were much less fluid, so that it appeared at times that the tool was more in control than the operator. Recognizing his limitations, Ollie handed it back.

A whistle from the newly constructed rail station sounded, and people started heading toward the station. Ollie stopped one of the passersby to ask what all the commotion was about.

"The train from St. Maries is coming in and they'll need help unloading firefighting supplies," he said.

Ollie, Drew, and I joined the other men, women and children who were streaming toward the station, keeping our eyes on the stretch of rail that followed the river's curves, then disappeared into a tunnel. We watched for the puff of black smoke that would signal the train's arrival. The weight of imminent danger dragged on everyone's faces and spirits.

The black nose of the train's engine emerged from the tunnel's black void, pulling behind it a half dozen box cars and two windowed crew cars. Seeing so many cars was a welcome sight to everyone there.

Fifteen minutes later the train had come to a stop and the doors of the boxcars were opened, revealing an ample supply of goods, dry and fresh. Ollie spotted a stack of supplies from his parents' mercantile, including four sacks of hand-crushed flour that we had prepared for graduation. One of the crew cars emptied out more than a dozen men, while the other one remained closed. Everything had been unloaded within an hour, with wagons and pack teams sent out to their destinations. Two business-types had gotten off the train, most likely representatives from the government or Forest Service. Avery's two Forest Service rangers briefed them, their jaws tight.

We loaded the last wagon with goods from the train as darkness began to overtake the town. The train fired its boilers, readying itself for the trip over Lolo Pass and into Montana. Workers unhooked the last crew car which still hadn't been opened, baiting our curiosity. The engine churned black smoke out of its charred stack and headed east. We strolled down to the loading dock of the depot, approaching the lone crew car that was left behind. About twenty feet away we could see silhouettes of men walking around. Suddenly, someone stepped out of the shadows.

"That's close enough, men," he said. He carried a pistol strapped around his waist and had a badge pinned to his shirt that reflected the light of an overhead light post.

"Yes sir," Drew said and turned immediately around. I followed but Ollie didn't.

"What's so important about this car that it needs a guard, sir? Is the President in there or something?" Ollie craned his neck to get a view of the car's passengers. Drew and I stopped, just as curious as Ollie but not as bold.

The man put a cigar in his mouth and lit it. "Not quite," he laughed, blowing out a cloud of smoke. "These here are felons from St. Maries and Coeur d' Alene. They'll be working on a crew to help fight the fire. Until then, they stay locked up right here."

Drew took a step back toward the crew car. "You said from St. Maries, sir?"

"That's right. We emptied the jail, save for a couple killers. By my estimation, these guys will be the best fire fighters on the job."

Drew took another step forward so he was alongside Ollie.   Both   watched   the   curtained windows of the car's interior.

"Sir, are you familiar with a man named—" Drew stopped as the curtain inside the crew car drew back. There, staring out from his prison on wheels, was Batum Schrag.

Chapter 22

"Do you think he saw you?" Ollie asked as we hurried from the crew car.

"I don't know. The lamp wasn't very bright," Drew said. "And he wouldn't be looking for us, anyhow." Still, Drew's voice was nervous. And rightly so.

We spent the rest of the evening at Edward Pulaski's tent, learning the wily habits of forest fires and how to fight them. We were joined by a dozen other men who had arrived on the train a few hours earlier, weak from their journey but intent on learning everything they could. We were taught how to make a fire line using the pulaski; where and how to seek refuge if overcome by flames; and how to signal each other in the midst of a fire. We were also given a crude map of the different camps that had been established and an overview of the plan that was devised to manage the fires that were known. The reality of the moment had set in.

A man in the back of the tent stood to address Edward and the government official with him. "How's this fire compare to the Hinckley fire over in Minnesota? My uncle fought that fire in '94 and said he ain't seen nothing like it."

"As far as acres burned, we're quickly approaching their mark of 160,000," the official answered. "Fortunately, we don't have the population around the burn area that they did. They lost a dozen towns—as far as we can tell, only a few of our towns are currently in danger."

"If we've already lost that kind of acreage, why in the hell is it we're just getting word of how bad it is?"

The official set his jaw and shook his head. "Listen, men, I know you're angry. This land is your livelihood.   But   considering   each   ranger   is responsible for over a quarter-million acres, that don't give us much of an edge on Mother Nature. We do what we can."

Edward interrupted. "The weather service says there's no relief in sight. We're about 80% beneath our average rainfall for this time of year. And with two or three new fires breaking out each day, there's no time for second guessing."

"Is more help on the way?"

"The unofficial word is that United States soldiers are being put on standby in case they're needed. And, as most of you men know, the word is out to all parts to send as many able bodies as possible.   You'll get a briefing after breakfast regarding other details. Any more questions?"

"Just one," asked one man. "How many have you lost so far?"

"None," answered Edward. "And that's how we want to keep it."

With that, the training was over and the group dismissed. Some men hung around and asked more questions of the government official, but most were ready to bed down and get as much sleep as their nerves would allow. Jacob was waiting just outside the tent door when we came out.

"So, ready to hit the fire trails, boys?" he asked.

"I've been ready for a year," Ollie said. "I'd head out tonight if someone was kind enough to point me in the right direction."

Jacob laughed. "You'll be pointed just following breakfast. Until then, let's head for my bunk and we'll get the three of you settled. I got your horses over to the stable. They'll be fine until morning."

As we made our way out of the lit streets and toward Jacob's bunk, the haze became more evident, stifling the moon's glow and dimming the little light cast from occasional lanterns hanging in tent doorways. A light layer of ash from burning timber was beginning to settle around and every time you took a breath you tasted the fire.

When we reached Jacob's bunk he told us to throw our bedrolls wherever they would fit. "Sister Louisa will have breakfast ready at sunrise," he said, "so you best be getting some sleep while you can."

I'm not sure what went through Drew and Ollie's minds, because we didn't speak. But sleep was the last thing on my mind.

Jacob woke me, packing up his bedroll before the sun was more than a faint glow silhouetting the tent. "You still have an hour until breakfast, Jackson," he whispered, tying his bootlaces. "Might as well get some rest."

"Naw, my blood is rushing already," I said. "Reckon I'll get up and head into town to see if I can lend a hand."

"I'll be down at the livery if you don't find any takers." He ducked out of the tent and into the dawning sky. I followed, rolling my bedroll and tucking it into my pack. I slipped on my boots without stirring Drew and Ollie.

The trail leading to town was no wider than a stock wagon. It was bordered on either side with tents spaced at regular intervals. At first, most of the tents were vacant, set up in anticipation of incoming firefighters. As we got closer, some showed signs of people stirring, while others were silent, the occupants sleeping in the face of the day's threat. I passed Edward Pulaski's empty tent and continued into town, where men were gathered on the street corners. The combination of light and smoke made them into apparitions. Passing by, I overheard their conversations. One group wondered whether their supervisor was part of a union, another was comparing pay rates among newcomers, and a third was debating the benefits of lighting a backfire.

When I got to the livery, I found Jacob who had his hands full shoeing a mule from one of the pack teams. "Jackson, give me a hand, will you?" he said. "This is one time I can appreciate what Handy has to go through. Funny thing is, Handy can curse through the whole thing and light a cigarette at the same time." I steadied the mule so Jacob could continue.

"Any word whether things have gotten worse?" I asked.

"Not in the mood for small talk? Can't say I blame you." Jacob finished nailing the shoe then dropped the hoof. "No word yet, but then I can't say I expected any different. As dry as it is out there, only bad news is going to be easy to come by. We're in for the fight of our life."

Watching the sun rise over town, I wished he would have lied. Fear was quickly outweighing my anticipation.

Drew and Ollie joined us at breakfast where Sister Louisa performed a miracle with food for the forty or so men who were present. The main course was some sort of gravy-covered hash topped with fried eggs, accompanied by fresh baked bread and half a dozen different preserves. We feasted until it hurt. One of the government officials from the night before stood up to address the crowd.

"We just received word from a lookout," he said, his face as somber as the moment. "The wind started gusting last night this side of the Montana border and has continued. One report said that the fire was throwing burning embers up to a mile and a half away. These embers have started over a dozen new fires in the last twenty-four hours alone. Should this continue, we'll have a disaster of biblical proportions on our hands. This beast must be stopped, gentlemen." Knives, forks and dishes stopped rattling and conversation stalled. "If the land you've come to know and rely on is to be preserved, it will be due to your efforts in this crisis. If you have a back, use it; if you're good with your mind, engage it; if you have a skill or trade, exercise it; and above all else, if you have an 'in' with the Almighty, now would be a good time to see if He's listening."

Each team boss joined the government official as they read from a roster, assigning each man to a crew. Drew, Ollie and I were called to Edward's crew, along with Jacob. The rangers that had been stationed at Avery called out our destinations.

"Edward, you take your men toward Marble Creek. Word has it that with the wind gusting, the drainage is a prime target for the fire." Edward spun on his heels and headed for the door. Drew, Ollie, Jacob and I followed along with two other men I didn't know.

When we hit the front steps of the cookhouse, Edward spoke over his shoulder, "Each of you grab an axe at the blacksmith's, gather your personal goods together, and meet me at the livery stable in ten minutes."

Jacob already had a pulaski, so he went directly to the livery. The rest of us stopped over at the blacksmith's where we saw the little boy from the night before. "Are you headin' out?" he called to us. "You are, aren't you? I'm tellin' my pa I'm goin' with. I don't care what he says."

"Listen, little man," Drew said. "When we get back into town, I'll tell you all about the fire and how we fought it with the tools you and your pa made. Is it a deal?"

The boy kicked the dirt and threw an imaginary rock. "I reckon so."

The pulaskis were lined up in front of the shop, each with a sanded pine handle, sharpened ax and opposing hoe blades. Each of us picked up one after another until we discovered the one right for us, and then stopped at Jacob's tent to fetch our packs and supplies. On the way back to the livery, we strutted along the dust-ridden road with our packs slung over one shoulder and our pulaskis over the other. I imagined it was how soldiers must have felt as they headed off to war, embarking on a mission to defend country, family, and honor at all cost. It encouraged me to think we were marching out as heroes. Or at least it helped me mask the terror I felt at what we were about to do.

"You men get your horses ready and meet the rest of us at the trailhead south of town," Edward directed as we approached the stable. He looked even more hurried than usual. "I just received word from a messenger who rode all night to get here that the fire took its first victims. Some homesteaders between here and the Montana border were trying to save their house and barn. Wiped out the whole family."

We stood expressionless. I thought of the Johannesons who had hewn their existence from the land, only to see it turn on them. I envisioned countless other families scattered throughout the valleys of northern Idaho and western Montana. All of a sudden their lives, too, became important.

"Best get going," Jacob said as he finished saddling his horse. "Edward waits for no one. And believe me, you don't want to be caught in a firestorm without him."

We hustled with our packs and saddles and followed Jacob out of the stable, making our way past other crews hurrying to get ready. Supplies were doled out according to how large each crew was and how far they had to travel. Talk was limited to the business of fire fighting, replacing the more common conversations about booze, whores, timber size, logging practices and where to find a decent camp cook.

"How many are you feeding out of your camp, Schilling?" asked a red-headed Irishman who was managing the distribution of goods.

"Five of us are heading out this morning, but we're joining a crew over in the Clearwater drainage. If my information is right, they're about a dozen strong."

"What about Edward's old camp?" asked the Irishman. "Are you meeting up with them? They're up that way as well."

"I'm leading that crew." We looked around to see the gentleman with a badge who had been guarding the crew car full of convicts the night before. "They'll be helping me keep an eye on my jailbirds." He chuckled. "If all goes right, maybe the fire'll get them." No one responded to his humor. Instead, the red-headed man nodded, satisfied. The guard continued. "All the same, if Edward's crew could drop off some supplies to his old camp along the way, I'd be much obliged. He's sure to get there faster than me, since I have these chained maggots to deal with."

Jacob and the Irishman agreed. We loaded our horses with sacks of flour, a side of cured ham, dried corn and some cans of vegetables. Sister Louisa stepped out of the cookhouse long enough to give us a flour sack full of leftovers from breakfast.

"It won't get you far, but at least you'll have it for a couple days." She gave Jacob a kiss on the cheek and each of us a wink. "When you get back I'll fry you each a steak fit for royalty."

Jacob strapped the sack of bread with the rest of the supplies and gave his horse a whack. "That'll do us," he said. "Let's head for the trail."

Ollie and I jerked our horses around and fell in behind him, while Drew struggled with the extra pack horse in tow.

The man with the badge yelled to his crew behind us. "You men get these things loaded. I want to be on the trail within an hour. If I hear one complaint I'll strap you to a nearby tree and leave you there for the fire or cougars. Whichever one gets you first makes no difference to me."

The sound of chains rattling and metal colliding got our attention. Ollie and I turned around to watch the convicts loading supplies. They were joined in pairs, linked by a single shackle attached to their ankles. Drew, still battling with the extra packhorse for control, was on the edge of their group and unaware. The packhorse dropped its head and reared back on its hind legs. A couple of the pots and pans loosened and fell.

"If you can't handle the animal you don't belong here." At first it was hard to tell where the voice had come from. From where Ollie, Jacob and I stood, it looked as if there were about thirteen men. Then the group parted, revealing the source. It was Batum Schrag. "We don't need boys up here," he said. "We need men, you good for nothing."

Drew bent down and picked up the pans. Ollie let go of his horse's reins and started at Batum. Jacob reached out and grabbed his shirt, pulling him back into place. "Stay put, little man. This is one squabble you don't want your nose in."

"I'm speaking to you, boy," Batum continued. "What in the hell are you doing here?"

The guard kicked the chain between Batum and his fellow convict. "Shut that mouth of yours. You'll speak only when I say so." He cocked back his arm and backhanded Batum, whose complexion darkened with rage. The guard spoke to Drew. "Now listen, youngster, get your horses and get up there with Pulaski, understand?"

Drew got out a faint, "Yes sir," without taking his eyes from Batum.

Ollie shrugged himself loose from Jacob's grip to meet Drew as he approached.   Drew continued past Ollie, then Jacob, and then me, on toward the trailhead.

Batum called after him. "Be lookin' over your shoulder, Featherweight, 'cause when you least expect it, I'll be there, you son-of-a-bitch."   The statement was followed by more sharp words from the guard man and a loud slap. Then silence.

Chapter 23

Drew kept well in front of Jacob, Ollie and me even after we joined up with Edward Pulaski. Any other day, Andrew Featherweight would never have been so bold as to take the lead. But this was no ordinary day. We were being transformed from boys to men, preparing to battle a fire.

The early morning passed with nothing more than an increase in smoke. Occasionally we'd enter a clearing and catch a glimpse of the slowly blackening sky, but saw nothing in the way of actual flames. I was getting anxious, wanting to encounter some action. I was ready to meet the enemy but the enemy was avoiding me. In fact, according to my sense of direction we were headed away from the fire, which did nothing to encourage my effort. My pulaski was starting to bruise my shoulder and my legs were aching from Edward's quick pace. My thoughts quickly drifted back to Pa's suggestion of a week in Coeur d' Alene sunning by the lake. With every passing minute, my regret grew.

Edward and Drew had disappeared around the winding corners of the trail. Jacob and Ollie were in front of me conversing about the railroad and its impact on the mercantile. As for me, I was concentrating on overcoming the discomfort in my shoulder and legs. They had told us at camp not to put our fire fighting tools on our horses so we'd still be able to fight the flames in case the horses were spooked by the fire and ran off. Still, seeing that we weren't even in sight of the fire and my shoulder was rubbed raw, I decided to go against their advice. I slipped my pulaski into the pack strapped to my horse. I determined that as we came upon any flames, I would hoist it back onto my shoulder. In the meantime, it was a welcome relief.

The sun had long since stolen the cool morning air, leaving the afternoon stale and hot. The added combination of trail dust, sweaty horses, and smoke left us with little reprieve. We continued until the sun was well overhead, then encountered Drew and Edward on the other side of a small rise.

"According to my estimation, we'll meet up with the other crew just before supper," Edward said. "They should be waiting for us. Once we arrive, we'll divvy up supplies, then head out right away to see if we can make our camp by nightfall. If not, we'll just have to do our best. Come get some of this grub Sister Louisa put together for us and we'll push on."

I let go of my horse's reins, grabbed as much food as my mouth and hands could hold, and sat on a fallen tree to enjoy a moment of rest. The others did the same except Edward, who wandered into the underbrush after throwing down a piece of bread and a cup of water.

After lunch, Jacob and Ollie continued to discuss economic changes throughout the St. Joe Valley like a couple of city councilmen, appearing no more exhausted from our journey than from a jaunt through the park.   But after a few minutes they settled against a tree and tipped their hats over their eyes. Drew on the other hand, got up and started cleaning out his horse's hooves, checking its shoes and rearranging his pack.   Though I would have liked to engage in clever conversation, or perform some care and maintenance on my horse, the food had taken its effect on me and quickly dulled my senses. I had just settled in near Jacob and Ollie when a shout rang out from the underbrush. It was Edward. "The flames are at my heels," he yelled. He crashed through a bush into our clearing. "Dig in, men. This is for your lives."

To be truthful, Edward's shouting didn't startle me as much as the fact that when I raised my head, I noticed that only Edward and Drew's horses were still nearby. I realized I hadn't tethered my horse in my haste for lunch.

Drew and Edward grabbed their pulaskis and rapidly dug a fire line, using the tool's sharp edge to cut through tree roots and its opposing end to hoe a line through the topsoil. Jacob and Ollie, who were caught off guard as I was, sprang up and paced about, unsure what to do.

"Grab your tools and get busy. Those flames won't wait for you to make up your mind or whatever the hell you're doing." Edward barked.

Jacob and Ollie looked at one another, then at me. Ollie dropped to his knees and started frantically digging with his bare hands. Jacob ran up and down the trail looking for his horse while simultaneously kicking at the dirt in a feeble effort to loosen the soil. I broke a limb off a nearby tree and jabbed at the ground, accomplishing about as much as Ollie and Jacob were. After a few frantic moments, I looked up, expecting flames to be lapping at my face. But what I saw was Drew and Edward calmly resting against their pulaskis. Seeing this, I slowed my reckless digging, which got Ollie and Jacob's attention as well.

"Your horses are about 20 yards into the brush where I hid 'em," Edward said. "Once you've retrieved them, make an effort to keep up." He slung his pulaski over his shoulder and headed down the trail. Drew fell in behind. I dropped my stick, Ollie rose from his knees, and Jacob, Ollie, and I ventured into the woods to retrieve our horses. We each pulled our pulaskis from our packs and slung them over our shoulders without speaking a word.

Our break-neck pace must have exceeded even Edward's expectations, as we met up with his old camp by three o'clock that afternoon. I was taken aback by their appearance. Here were men who had actually seen flames. Fear was in their eyes, exhaustion in their bones, and defeat permeated their demeanors. The thirty or so men looked beaten.

"Listen up, men," Edward said, dismounting. "I know you've been out here for close to a month, and on behalf of the United States Forest Service I want to extend a thank you. Because of your efforts and those of many men like you, we've been able to hold the fire back in many critical areas. In fact, word has it we're close to having the whole thing under control and behind us." The crew's eyes widened a little. He shot a glance our way, and then back. "Still, we have to persevere so as to not let any new spot fires erupt. We aren't out of danger yet." Edward continued his speech as the four of us wandered away from the crew.

"Why did Edward tell them the fire was under control?" Drew asked after we were out of earshot.

"Did you see how they looked?" Jacob asked. "If he'd told them the worst was yet to come, they probably would have collapsed right there."

Edward wasted no time; as soon as we'd unloaded the supplies he told us to get ready to head out. "The crew of convicts should be here by noon tomorrow," he told the crew as we were leaving. "Keep your distance, but give the sheriff the help he needs keeping an eye on them. We'll be just over the top of the next ridge, concentrating our efforts to the west of Little Lost Lake and due south into the Clearwater drainage. I've left directions for you to go to Setzer Creek. Godspeed to you all."

We loaded the remaining supplies for our own camp onto the packhorse, which allowed us to mount our own horses, who groaned and grunted under our weight. Edward said he usually didn't ride his horse after a hard day's work, but under the time constraints, he thought it was more important to beat the sun into camp. Already the shadows of surrounding peaks were stretching into the valley and the cool air of evening pouring in. With it came the stench of stale smoke.

The forest closed in behind us as we departed. We left the valley floor, following the trail up the mountainside. Edward led the way followed by Drew, then Jacob, Ollie and me. We pressed on, traversing the steep slope to the Clearwater drainage on the other side.

Chapter 24

Not an hour out of camp we caught sight of a lone man walking toward us on the trail. The dim light of evening kept him disguised. His soot-covered features came into focus as he approached. Edward recognized him. "Where's your crew, Will?" he asked.

He couldn't, or wouldn't, talk. Instead he just stood there, eyes empty and jaw set.

"You were supposed to wait for us in the Clearwater drainage." Edward dismounted and came up alongside him. "Where's your crew, man?"

Will looked right through him. "The demon got them, I guess." A slight breeze picked up, sending a rustle through the underbrush and a shudder clear through me.

"Did they make it out of the drainage? Is there anyone behind you?" Edward squinted down the trail, straining to see if others were following. He turned back toward Will. "Dammit, man. What happened?"

Jacob swung down and took his water sack to Will, lifting it for him to drink. He grabbed Jacob to steady himself, exposing blistered hands. The sores were open and festering and remnants of crude bandages stuck to them. Water dribbled down his front, soaking a soiled tourniquet that was draped around his leg. Without a word we understood his story.

When Will finally let the water sack drop from his lips he could only say: "the flames were everywhere."

Ollie, Drew and I got off our horses and gathered around. Edward paced back and forth in front of Will, barking questions until he realized that he was getting nowhere. He turned his back in frustration.

"Is your last name Johanneson, sir?" Drew asked gently. Edward looked around for Will's response: his eyes lit up like a candle.

"On our way up to Avery we spent the night at your homestead," Drew said. "Your wife asked us to give you this note if we saw you." Drew reached inside his pocket and pulled out the letter. "They're all just fine, sir. Your family's just fine."

Will took the letter with shaky hands and opened it. After reading a few lines, he dropped his head and started to cry.

Edward took the opportunity to continue his inquiry. "Will, we need to know where the rest of your crew is and the status of the fire. Can you help us?"

The letter must have pulled him back to some sense of reality, as he was able to put thoughts together. "We split up—sometime around noon—the flames were too intense."

"Where at, Will? Where were the flames so intense?"

Will paused. "About ten miles on other side of the ridge. But they're coming this way. There's no escaping them, Edward. I tell you, it's a demon."

"And you have no idea about the others?"

Will shook his head. "It was by the grace of God I happened on this trail. No telling what happened to the others."

Edward looked hard at Will, then up the trail. "Jacob," he said, "you take Will back to camp. We'll continue on to see if we can find anyone else. Tomorrow morning, at first light, get that crew on the trail to join us. Depending on how bad the fire looks, we'll either make our way down to the Clearwater drainage or stay on top of the ridge. We'll leave a sign on the trail for you. Leave two men behind at camp: one to wait for the sheriff and his convicts and the other to take Will back to Avery."

Jacob helped Will onto his horse and then turned back toward us. "I'll be seeing you tomorrow, I reckon," he said, nodding and then pivoting his horse around toward the valley below.

We mounted our horses and continued the climb to the ridgeline, where the demon patiently awaited our arrival.

By the time we reached the ridgeline, the dim light of evening had faded into night. As we crested the top, we entered a clearing that gave us a view of the valleys on either side. North and to our left, in the St. Joe Valley, hundreds of yellow and orange lights dotted the landscape. South and to our right the Clearwater drainage mimicked the St. Joe except with larger and brighter fires. I felt as if we were sitting in heaven and peering down at the earth below. That far removed, the beauty of fantasy overshadowed its horror. We sat there a few moments as the moon illuminated all it could through the smoke.

"There's enough light to continue if we stay on top of this ridge," Edward said. We'll head west toward Little Lost Lake. By the look of it, I doubt the rest of Will's crew is still in the valley. And if they are, that's where they'll stay." Edward pulled his horse's reins and headed west as he'd said. Drew, Ollie and I did the same, weary and weak from the day.

I must have dozed off in my saddle somewhere between midnight and dawn. I was startled awake when my horse stopped. Edward,

Drew and Ollie were talking. As I came to my senses, their words started to become clear.

"If my estimations are right, we should be about halfway between where we started and Little Lost Lake. By the look of the sky, we have three or four hours before dawn." Edward dismounted. "Let's bed down here. Our horses could use the rest."

Edward said he would sleep light enough to keep us out of danger, which made no difference to me. As soon as my head touched the ground I was fast asleep.

A firm push from Edward's boot woke me. The cool morning air was laced with smoke. It stung our lungs. The sun hadn't yet broken over the horizon, but it was threatening. Edward had a small cookfire going and some coffee perking over the flames. He poured us each a cup.

"After we're packed up, we'll continue toward Little Lost Lake. I know a clearing with a spring running through it. We'll set-up central camp there."

We sat in silence, sipping our coffee, its strong and bitter taste hopelessly lost in the smell of nature's inferno. Edward threw the dregs from his coffee cup on the fire and stood up, his legs stiff. He shook them out and rubbed them violently, then headed to a nearby rock above camp where he could get a view of the valleys. Ollie, Drew and I continued to nurse the coffee trickling down our throats into tight and empty stomachs. It was the first time we'd been left alone since our last night in Avery.

"You guys alright?" I asked.

"I'm okay," Drew said, bringing his cup to his lips. He kept his gaze on the cookfire's weak flames. Ollie just shrugged.

"I'm fine," I said, nodding to convince myself. I figured I should say something else since I had posed the question in the first place. Truth was, I wanted them to say how scared they were so that I could admit it, too. Instead, we each steeped in our own ghosts and fears. The sound of Edward shuffling back down from his viewpoint broke our silence.

"I reckon we've been here long enough," he said. Let's get on the trail."

We doused the fire with the remaining coffee and spaded dirt over its coals. Edward suggested we lead the horses for an hour so they could warm up their muscles. To be honest, the horses' health was the last thing on my mind. Had Edward not been intimidating with his 'suggestions' I might have ignored him and climbed on my horse. But Edward was our lifeline to survival, which meant his way was our way.

That first hour went by slowly, taking us over the steepest, most uneven terrain we'd seen. We traversed hills as steep as a cow's face without adequate light. Loose rocks made our footing uncertain. By the time we finally mounted our horses, the sky was dazzling with colors over the eastern range, the sunrise filtered by dense smoke.

As we rode the ridgeline west, we could see stretches of the fire's path in the adjoining valleys below. The dry, parched fields on the slopes of the hills became immediate fuel. The fire gained momentum from these tinder-patches to engulf the surrounding trees. From there, even a light wind could toss the flames to new patches of timber. Across the horizon we saw a storm front looming, promising either fire-quenching rain or simply lightning. As we rode, we watched the storm front driving clouds through the layers of smoke that settled in the valley floor and spiraled into the morning sky.

Chapter 25

The warm morning had turned into a hot mid-day by the time we reached the meadow Edward had described. A small stream ran along its northern edge and then past to Little Lost Lake, which was still five miles further west and out of sight. By lunchtime, we had set up camp, complete with a four-walled canvas sleeping tent, a crude cooking pit, and a formidable latrine Drew and Ollie made from scavenged timbers. When we were finished, we sat on the ground around the fire pit and started gnawing on jerked beef and corn bread.

"Assuming the winds don't change course, we should be out of the fire's way here," Edward said. He grabbed a walking stick from the pile of branches we'd gathered for the cooking fire, slung his pulaski over his shoulder, and took off walking south. The three of us looked at one another, wondering if we should follow.

"Are we to join you, sir?" asked Ollie.

"Can if you want. I'm going to see if there's any sight of Will Johanneson's crew."

Ollie and Drew jumped to their feet, cramming lunch in their pockets as they grabbed for their pulaskis.

"You coming, J.D.?" Ollie asked, striding to keep up with Drew.

"Sounds like it's optional.   This meadow grass sure makes a fine bed," I said.

Ollie grunted and disappeared into the woods with the other two, leaving me alone in the meadow. My mind stilled as my eyes closed. I stayed that way for a few moments until my mind suddenly snapped awake: I was a day and a half from Avery, in a forest that was being consumed by fire, and was soon to be joined by a crew of convicts. Suddenly sleep lost its appeal.

I decided to do some menial chores, like filling the water sacks from the stream, gathering more wood for the cooking fire, and making some structural improvements to Drew and Ollie's latrine. I wished I had taken Edward up on his invitation as I found myself frequently looking over my shoulder, listening for men's voices or a crackling fire in the distance. Along with the ever-increasing awareness that the fire might come barreling over the surrounding ridge any minute, I found the majority of my time alone to be anything but restful.

Despite my erratic and paranoid behavior, I finally pulled up a rock next to the creek for a moment of rest. I cupped my hands and dipped them into the cool water. Then, I lifted my hands above the creek's surface and spread my fingers, letting the water cascade out. I did this a time or two, letting the water run through my fingers back into the creek. Water was all we needed. But we needed so much more than my hands could carry. I dipped them again, this time bringing the water up to my mouth. Its coolness trickled down my throat inside and out, relieving the smoke, sun and heat.

The rustle of feet startled me and I looked up to see Jacob, the sheriff, and his crew of convicts lumber into camp. They were followed by a string of pack mules loaded with supplies. I motioned to Jacob as he scanned the site. "You've arrived," I said. "Everything go alright?" He pulled up a seat next to me.

"Other than those sonofabitchin' convicts, it all went smooth. Where are the others?"

"Edward led them off to look for some of Will's crew and to do some fire watch. They've been gone nearly four hours, I reckon. I can't imagine Drew and Ollie would miss supper. Edward, on the other hand, who knows." Jacob got down on his hands and knees to dip his face in the creek.

"Edward's pace damn near killed me. I think he had more concern for the horses than he did us."

Jacob came up and shook his head, sending water droplets flying. "You can talk, the horses can't. I'm sure he did the right thing." So much for a concerned listener. Jacob stood up and pulled his shirt tail out of his trousers to wipe off the rest of the water.

"Give us a hand unpacking the mule team, will you J.D.?"

"Sure thing, Jacob."

The sheriff had organized his crew and appeared to have everything under control without our help. Still, Jacob worked his way into the group and pitched in. I did the same, shouldering up next to a probable felon who would rather spit on me as look at me. Once the goods started coming off the mules and into my hands, though, I was consumed by work and forgot about my cohorts. All except Batum. I could feel his steely glare without even turning his way. I made every effort to avoid eye contact as we finished unpacking the team.

Edward, Drew and Ollie showed up just as we had unloaded the last mule. They looked tired and apparently hadn't found any of Will's crew. The sheriff split the convicts up into two groups. One distributed supplies to the areas where each walled tent would be erected. The other was put in charge cooking. Everyone included, there were almost fifty men in camp, and so living arrangements were rather involved. Four more wall tents were erected, the cooking area was increased, and another latrine was constructed. In no time a miniature community was built, leaving room for more crews to come if the fire continued on its current course. Ollie, Drew and I grabbed our bedrolls and packs, then headed into our tent to get situated before supper.

"What'd you see up on the ridge?" I asked.

"No sign of Will's crew, if that's what you're wondering," replied Ollie. "It wasn't a pretty sight. The fire is past the North Fork of the Clearwater. That means there isn't much stopping it from coming up the southeastern slope of the ridge we were traveling earlier today. According to Edward, a good westerly wind would put us just north of the fire's path. I sure the hell hope he's right—I won't be getting a decent night's rest if he isn't."

Drew and I looked at Ollie in disbelief.

"How do you expect to get a good rest regardless?" I stammered.

"Exactly," Drew said, intensely. "We're in a battle zone, Oliver Hunt. Don't expect to relax, have fun, clown around or get a good night's sleep until this thing is out and we're back in St. Maries. Can you get that through your thick skull?"

Ollie opened his mouth to speak, then shut it and returned to unloading his pack and spreading out his bedroll.

"Did you see Batum when you got into camp?" I asked Drew.

"Wasn't looking for him. I figure if I keep my distance and he'll do the same."

"He hasn't in the past."

"What are you getting at, J.D.?"

"I'm not sure, Drew. All I know is that I've never seen so much hatred in one man and it appears he's aiming all of it at you. Doesn't that bother you?"

"He ain't nothing but a low-life convict," Ollie said. "Besides, those chains won't let him do much of anything. If anything it's Batum who should be keeping an eye out. One swing of my pulaski and he'll hit the ground for good!"

Ollie's banter didn't register with Drew.

I said, "I just think that you—all three of us for that matter—need to be wary of him, that's all."

Drew looked up from his unpacking. "I told you, J.D., I have no problem with him."

Supper tasted good, the first hot meal we'd had since we left Sister Louisa. We sat at a makeshift table supported by two stumps. The sheriff made the convicts eat in a separate area so as not to bother the rest of us. Two men from Edward's old crew served the meal, while Edward and Jacob strategized about the days to come.

"When we left the old camp, two men who'd been with the sheriff since Avery said they'd send more supplies in a week," Jacob said. "We sent Will back with them. They also said two more crews would be joining us. They'll operate out of here, but concentrate their efforts to the north, in the St. Joe drainage. The forest ranger said an alternative camp could be Setzer Creek."

"I know that area well," Edward replied. "My only concern is that if the fire picks up momentum, Setzer Creek is quite a ways into the valley. Getting out of there in an emergency would be nearly impossible. When those other crews get here we'll make that call." Jacob nodded in agreement. "Tomorrow, I'll take these three and half the convicts west toward Little Lost Lake to start a fire line. There's an opening there I think will work as a natural fire-break. We'll also see if there's a location that will work for a backfire. You take the sheriff and the other half of the convicts and head over the ridge toward the Clearwater River. I'll draw you a map so you can dig a fire line there. When the rest of the men show up, they can look for Will's crew and identify potential backfire areas."

We sat at the supper table for two hours, listening to Edward's tactics for outsmarting the fire. It seemed he had a dozen solutions for every possible route the fire might take. He talked about how the fire sometimes rushed over the crowns of trees and stole oxygen from the forest floor— the principle behind lighting a backfire and robbing the oncoming fire of fuel and oxygen; how to get the most out of a team approach to digging a fire line; and how to read a fire's direction based on weather patterns. He was truly a master of the art of fire fighting. The sun was quickly waning when we finally pushed away from the table.

"Get a good night's rest, boys. We'll be heading out before dawn." Edward rose to his feet, stretching his legs. "If there's one thing you don't want to be without when you're fighting a fire, it's rest." He left us there, the three of us and Jacob, full of ideas about how the days would progress.

"Tomorrow's got to be the day," Ollie said when Edward was out of earshot. "I don't think I can go one more day without actually fighting the fire. I swear, if they even let me piss in the cooking pit, it would be a start." Even Drew chuckled at that one.

"I know what you mean," I said. "All the talk and anticipation is wearing me out. I think some hand-to-hand combat might actually be a relief."

"By the looks of what we saw this afternoon, we'll get plenty of action," Drew said. "I know Edward is thinking we're not in the fire's path, but I'm not so sure. I remember fighting a brush fire three years ago on our homestead. My uncle swore he knew which way the fire would go, so we put all our efforts into saving the garden. But the fire turned on us for no apparent reason and headed straight for the house. Had it not been for a fallow field between our homestead and the flames, we'd have lost everything."

"Nothing's for sure, Andrew," Jacob said, "but Edward's estimation of what might happen is the most accurate we're going to get. The rangers over in Avery aren't going to bring much help. Which reminds me: the two men who came with the sheriff said your Pa has been doing a great job supplying the efforts, Oliver." He reached into his pocket, pulled out a large envelope, and handed it to Ollie. "This came with the last shipment."

Ollie flipped the letter over in his hands. It was well stuffed. Drew, Jacob and I watched curiously. Ollie flipped it over a couple more times, then opened it slowly. He pulled out three smaller envelopes and handed one to each of us according to the names printed on them.

My envelope contained a letter from my parents, encouraging me to be careful and stay close to experienced firefighters. My Pa said my brothers would be at Avery within a few days by rail, since they'd just returned from logging a parcel west of St. Maries and had heard news of the fire. Mrs. Hunt had also included a note reminding us she'd be praying for us and asking Drew and me to watch out for Oliver. After I'd finished reading, I put the papers back in the envelope and slipped it into my bib pocket.

"What'd yours say?" I asked Ollie.

Ollie had one sheet of paper cast aside and was intently reading another. I snatched the discarded sheet. It was from his parents. The one he was reading was undoubtedly from Phoebe. I looked over at Drew, who had turned away from the table.

"You okay, Drew?" I asked.

"Fine," he mumbled.

Jacob and I looked at each other. "Is that from Anna?" I asked. He nodded. Ollie continued reading, fingering a photo that had been enclosed. When he finally finished, he passed around the picture.

"It's the one my Ma took of me and Phoebe." Had he been a peacock, he would have been in full bloom. "And this here letter is from Phoebe herself. Damn, boys, I think she's fallen for me."

Drew still hadn't turned back, but continued to read, supporting his head with one hand, holding the paper with the other. Ollie went so far as to say Phoebe would be lucky to have a man like him around for the rest of her life. Oliver Hunt, the same man who in the morning couldn't decide where he'd be at lunch, was talking about a lifetime with a woman. The only thing that I could guess was that he'd been breathing too much smoke.

Drew finished and stood up neatly folding the letter back into the pocket of his trousers.

"Where're you off to, Drew?" Ollie asked. He didn't say anything but wandered into the middle of camp with his head down. "What's the matter with him? I'm finding out." Ollie swung his legs around and hopped off the bench.

"Now is probably not a good time, Ollie," Jacob said. "Looks like he wants to be alone." If it would've been me speaking, Ollie would have simply continued on. But, since it was Jacob, he plopped back down on the table.

"He's just in such a stupor it's really starting to irritate me."

Suddenly we heard a scuffle break out on the other side of camp. Ollie was the first to his feet; Jacob and I followed close behind. When we got to the scene, Edward and the sheriff were holding Drew, who was struggling to get loose from their grip and re-engage with Batum, who was being restrained by three other men about ten feet away. They looked like a couple of rabid dogs, breathing erratically, cursing and snarling at each other. Ollie jumped toward the center of things, but Jacob muscled him back to the outer circle.

"This isn't your fight, little man," he whispered to Ollie.

"All of you, get back to whatever you were doing," Edward yelled. "The excitement's over. Get that sonofabitchin' convict back in his chains and secured." The men holding Batum did just that, but not without a struggle. Then, they chained him to a jackpine on the outskirts of the camp.

Edward turned to Drew, who had calmed down somewhat and was sitting on the ground. "What the hell got into you, son? You came at him unprovoked. I don't know what kind of bad blood you got between you, but if I see anything like that again, I'll put you in chains, too, understand?" Edward and the sheriff left Drew in our care and went off to deal with the rest of the crew.

Blood streamed down Drew's face from a cut below his left eye, and he was holding his stomach.

"I should have been there with you," Ollie said.

Drew looked up with an anger and terror in his eyes I'd never seen in any man, let alone Andrew Featherweight. "This isn't your matter, Ollie, so stay the hell out of it." He dropped his head back down catching his breath.

"What'd Anna say, Drew?"

There was a pause, then Drew started sobbing. It was faint at first but then it intensified. He said before they shipped the convicts out to fight the fire, Batum was escorted to his house to pick up some supplies. While the escorts waited in the wagon outside, Batum beat Anna with his bare fists.

He told her he'd have killed her if there weren't men waiting outside.

Jacob and Ollie helped Drew to his feet and dusted him off, then went to talk to Edward about keeping Batum in restraints at all times. I used a piece of my sleeve to try and stop Drew's bleeding then helped him hobble back toward the tent.

"J.D., I don't know what to do. If he lives, Anna's sure to suffer. If I kill him, then I'm no better than he is." He looked at me but I had no answers. His eyes blurred with tears.

Chapter 26

The next few days went off without a hitch, one just like the next. The sun continued its hot pursuit, blocked by layers of smoke which made the air continually harder to breathe, and the storm, with continued form, darkening the sky further. Ollie got his wish for action, as we encountered a few isolated brush fires, but nothing serious. Some of them, in fact, were no bigger than an out-of-control campfire. Blisters from our pulaskis' handles had come and gone, leaving open sores that made the work even more difficult. The days got longer as we ventured further from camp to survey the damage, make fire lines, and fight small flares. There wasn't an hour that went by I didn't wish we had gone west instead. But then, I reasoned, we'd probably have eventually made the trip to Avery to help out. Still, it would have been after a spell of fishing the banks of Lake Coeur d' Alene, lazily watching river boats, and finding trouble and adventure in town each night.

New crews began joining us each day, bringing reports of how the rest of the fire was shaping up. It was growing quickly, they said, fueled by dry conditions and driven by hot winds. With every report, Edward became more solemn and melancholy. He would talk with Jacob and the sheriff about plans and strategies, but didn't see it important to discuss matters with the rest of us. I figured he was trying to keep morale from dropping.

The morning of the fifth day, Drew, Ollie and I got ready to go with Edward and a dozen other men as we had every other day. We gathered around the table following breakfast, ready to head out.

"Boys," Edward said to the three of us, "you're on your own today. I'm taking most of the crew back into the St. Joe drainage to fight a main leg of the fire moving quickly down the valley toward Setzer Creek. If we can stop it, there's a chance we can save everything west of there. The three of you take off toward Little Lost Lake. There are a couple spot fires the lookouts reported. They shouldn't amount to much. Jacob's going with the sheriff and the convicts into the Clearwater drainage for a few days where they'll be digging a fire line. You'll be the only ones in camp until the other crews show up. If and when they do, take them with you. Jacob will come back even if the sheriff and the convicts stay in the Clearwater drainage. Wait for directions from him before you change any of your plans."

The three of us looked at each other unsure how to react. "Be careful, boys." "Sheriff," Edward continued, "put minimum restraints on your crew. They'll need all the mobility they can get."

"I'm not sure that's a good idea," the sheriff replied.

Edward took the sheriff by the arm. "If that fire is as out of control as I've been told, we don't want them burning to death on account of being chained to one another." Reluctantly, the sheriff agreed and had the men put in minimal restraints, which consisted of nothing more than ankle cuffs attached by a thin cable.

We had been within a couple miles of Little Lost Lake on two of our outings with Edward, but hadn't seen it yet. And since it was just over two hours by foot, we needed to get started.

Drew took charge. "Ollie, you get the lunch sack and some supplies in case we have to stay over night. J.D., get the tools. I'll get one of the horses and meet you back here." Ollie and I looked at each other then went about following orders. Once we had assembled everything, we got ready to head west. Jacob caught up to us just before we left.

"There's been a slight change of plans. Edward and his crew are going to Setzer Creek as he said, and the sheriff is taking a crew and most of the convicts into the Clearwater. But I'll be hanging back with five or six convicts and another man to ready the camp. Word has it a crew of fifty is headed our way."

"Sure you don't want us to stick around and help you?" Ollie asked. "We'd be glad to."

"No, I'll be fine. I've got plenty of help. Just thought I'd let you know." He paused. "Looks like it's going to get worse boys—a lot worse."

The sheriff hollered to Jacob that his convicts were waiting. We took off west and Jacob returned. I looked over my shoulder toward camp as I brought up the rear of our three-man crew. Edward led the way north toward the St. Joe Valley; the sheriff ventured south to the Clearwater, his convicts in a uniform line. Like a scattering herd, we all left safety to cover more territory, forage and survive on our own.

It must have been noon by the time we reached the lake. We'd fought a few small fires along the way, but nothing that was too threatening. Still, Little Lost Lake was a welcome sight. The glassy surface of the water reflected the surrounding timbers. The dry grass bordering its shores was a stark contrast to its deep blue water. I remembered Mr. Miller's descriptions of the lake's beauty and decided he hadn't done it justice. The mountains' impending slopes cradled the lake, and the rocky crags topped with evergreens that encircled the lake seemed to protect us from harm. A breeze swirled, lessening the stench of smoke, and minimizing our fear of fire for a moment.

Drew dropped the reins of the horse as we stripped the clothes from our soot-covered, sweat-laden bodies. Ollie was the first one in the water. He dove in, surfacing a dozen yards from shore. Drew and I entered a little more gingerly, not knowing how cold the spring-fed lake would be. We both yelped, then dove in, knowing from experience it was the only way to get used to the chill. We surfaced gasping, invigorated. After catching my breath, I rolled over on my back so I could gaze up at the sky. The water covered my ears, leaving only my face exposed. Drew swam out to Ollie and dunked him a few times for good measure. Drew jabbed me as he swam up. I turned to get one ear out of the water to hear him. "Can you figure why there doesn't seem to be as much smoke here?"

"I'm not sure, but I think it might be some sort of inversion thing. The bowl the lake sits in might be making its own weather system."

"Sounds good to me. Whatever the hell it is, I sure like it."

I raised my head completely out of the water and joined Drew looking around at our surroundings. Suddenly Ollie, who had just made it to shore, yelled, "There it is!" Drew and I looked to where he was pointing, alarmed. "The big tamarack Mr. Miller said he buried his brother under. That's got to be it."

Sure enough. Standing out like a royal bride among peasants was a mammoth tamarack at the south end of the lake, the deep contours of its red bark revealing age and longevity. Many of its branches were larger than the surrounding tree trunks, its boughs reaching out and covering its kingdom. It had to be the one.

"When you hawn-yawks get out, we'll go over and look for the grave. Maybe dress it up a bit for Mr. Miller. I think that'd be a fine thing to do." He looked at us from shore, his red hair glistening in the sun above and sporting a wide smile.

"He can sure be a bother at times, but I'm glad he's our friend," Drew said. I smiled in agreement. Ollie's little white behind was a humorous sight as he hopped from leg to leg, trying to avoid the hazards on the way back to his clothes. Drew and I eventually went back to floating and drifting about as if we had nothing else to do with only the sound of our breathing. We floated for what seemed a long time.

"Did you say something?" Drew asked me.

I raised my head. "No, did you?"

We looked toward shore to see if Ollie was trying to get our attention. He was nowhere in sight.

"Ollie," Drew shouted."

We waited for a reply. None came. Drew pulled his legs underneath him and swam for shore.

I followed. Drew had his trousers on and was pulling up his suspenders when I hit the shore. I grabbed my clothes and was wiping the water off when we both heard it: a rumble like a far-off herd of buffalo stampeding. As we continued to listen, the slight breeze stalled to a frightening standstill. The air grew stale and the smoke curled in. The noise continued. I jumped into my clothes.

"Ollie! Where are you?" Drew yelled as he ran to the horse. "Ollie!"

The horse was uncertain and jittery, prancing around and eluding Drew's efforts to grab her reins. Finally he was able to control the animal and unstrap our pack. He tied the horse to a nearby tree and grabbed our pulaskis, tossing me mine. Ollie's was missing. The rumble grew until it was deafening.

"Oliver Hunt!" Drew hollered into the woods. "If this is a joke, I swear I'll beat you within an inch of your life!"

"No need. I took care of him for you." The voice came from our left. We jerked our heads around and there was Batum Schrag, not more than twenty feet away. "And it was my pleasure. One less smart ass in the world." The cable connecting his ankle cuffs was severed, and he was casually leaning against a jack pine, twirling a pulaski in his hands, its blade red with blood. Ollie came staggering out from behind a bush. He was holding his stomach with one hand, blood streaming all around it. He looked up at Drew and collapsed to the ground.

"The little bastard won't die." Batum started to stride toward Ollie, who was between him and Drew. He lifted his pulaski but Drew's blocked him. I ran up beside.

"You son-of-a-bitch." Drew's arms twitched as he fingered the handle of his pulaski. "Get ready to rot in hell!"

With a swift stroke he lunged toward Batum, but was off balance enough that all Batum had to do was jab him in the side with his handle and send Drew sprawling. I took a swing with my pulaski, but was no match for Batum's experience and strength. He easily ducked and hit me directly in the legs with the blunt end of the hoe. I heard a bone snap and a shot of pain sent me to the ground. No sooner had I fallen than Batum was on his feet ready to strike again. But my little diversion had given Drew enough time to recover. He let loose a powerful blow that hit Batum in the right arm, laying open flesh and muscle. Batum dropped his pulaski from his limp right hand and whirled around to catch Drew with his left fist, sending him back to the ground. Batum leapt before Drew could recover, pummeling him with his left fist while blood gushed from the slash on his right arm.

I dragged myself a couple of feet and sat helpless next to Ollie, skewered just below the knee. Ollie was moaning, occasionally blacking out. I kept pressure on his wound with the shirt I hadn't had time to put on. The rumble in the distance and the density of smoke were increasing at an alarming rate. I found some rocks nearby and planned to throw them at Batum, but he and Drew were so entwined that I could have easily hit either of them. All I could do was sit and watch.

Drew retaliated with a flurry of punches to Batum's face and managed to slip out from underneath. They ended up standing at the same time, each staggering to square off. Drew had his back toward me, making it impossible to launch my rocks. Both men's chests were heaving; Batum's limp arm hung by his side and Drew held his stomach. Each waited for the other to make a move, the two of them poised next to a small precipice that dropped about ten feet to the exit stream from the lake. The rumble of the fire echoed throughout the valley. Overhead the wind picked up, howling across the treetops. Drew finally took a swing at Batum, who side stepped and recoiled and slammed his fist into Drew's face. Drew staggered, but was able to get his bearings. He tagged Batum's chin and followed with a blow to his cheek. Batum lost his balance then his footing, as the dry soil gave way underneath, toppling him into the adjacent creek bed and out of my sight.   A scream of pain competed with the approaching rumble and then I heard nothing.

Drew bent cautiously over the edge of the precipice. The woods had become so loud I could barely think. I looked east toward camp and that's when I spotted it: coming at us like a charging bull was a wall of fire from the forest floor to the tree tops and beyond. It filled my vision. Drew looked up but quickly turned his attention back to where Batum had fallen. The flames were racing toward us but Drew didn't move, evidently listening to something Batum yelled up at him.

"Drew," I yelled, "what in the hell are you doing?" But he just stood there and stared. I took one of my rocks and threw it at him, hitting him in the leg. "Drew, we're going to burn to death! Get us to the lake!" He ignored me and tilted his head at the sky. Finally he walked past Ollie and me to the pack lying on the ground behind us and pulled out the burlap bag that held my pa's pistol.   Drew disappeared over the precipice and into the creek bed where Batum was lying. Burning embers had started to drop from the sky, igniting the grass and brush all around us. I let go of Ollie and dragged myself over to a nearby tree where I tried to reach a branch so I could stand up. A noise like a sharp clap of thunder came from the creek bed. I froze, watching the edge of the bank where Drew had disappeared. Embers continued to fall. Overhead, the treetops were engulfed in flames and were dropping branches to the forest floor. I trembled, my eyes darting between the ledge and Ollie, who continued to lie on the ground bleeding and moaning. Suddenly, a hand reached over, looking for something to grab onto. The hand found a sapling and Andrew Featherweight hoisted himself up.

"How's Ollie?" he asked, sober and fully aware.

"I'm not sure. He just groans. I think he's lost a lot of blood." It was difficult to talk over the fire. "What happened down there?"

He ignored my questions and looked down at my dangling leg. "How is it?"

"It hurts, but I'll live." A branch crashed not far from us. "Let's get to the lake."

Drew broke a branch and handed it to me for a crutch. I put my weight on it. Drew untied the horse, which was bucking and straining to get away from the approaching fire. He then hurried over to Ollie and gently cradled him, his motionless body limp in Drew's powerful arms. He waded into the lake, and I hobbled in after him, embers, burning branches and ash falling around us. When we hit the water, Ollie's blood spread across the surface of the lake like an oil spill, billowing from his wound. The three of us floated there in Little Lost Lake, watching the inferno engulf the surrounding forest. The air became stifling and difficult to breathe. Drew held Ollie close as he continued to moan and gasp for air.

"Come on, little man, stay with me," Drew shouted.

Ollie's eyes opened slightly. "Did you get him, Andrew?"

"I got him, Ollie."

Ollie closed his eyes for a moment then jerked them open. "Good going, you big ox." A faint smile drifted across his face. His eyes closed. We floated out into the middle of the lake, dipping beneath the water as often as possible to avoid the fire's heat.

Too much was happening around us; I never knew when Oliver Hunt took his last breath.

Drew and I found a fallen crag to hold onto as we floated with Ollie's limp body in the center of Little Lost Lake. My leg was throbbing and the deep crimson water relected the blood lost from the wounds Ollie and I had sustained. It seemed like a lifetime to wait as the fire continued to burn, skirting the edge of the lake and gulping underbrush and small trees with a seemingly unending appetite. Eventually the flames died down and we made our way out of the lake and on to the shore where the charred remains of the once lush forest continued to smoke and pop, trees dropping firey limbs on to the forest floor. The fire had been relentless but swift in devouring its fuel. Drew set Ollie's lifeless body on the ground and helped me prop myself against a rock. The soil was still warm to the touch. Drew took off his shirt and covered Ollie's face and chest. He went to the precipice and looked over the edge.

"Batum asked me to shoot him, J.D. Said he didn't want to burn to death."

Once again Drew looked to me for answers. This time I had one. "The bastard deserved to die, Andrew. I'm sorry it had to be you, though."

The encounter with Batum and the fire must have distracted us from the reality that our best friend's dead body was lying a few feet away, as neither Drew nor I had anything to say.

We hadn't been out of the water more than a few minutes when we heard more branches snapping. Drew took out the gun that was stuck in his waistband. We both peered through the trees.

"Drew, Ollie, J.D? Anyone here?" It was Jacob.

"Over here," Drew said.

Jacob hurried over. As soon as he saw us he stopped and readied his gun. "What happened to you?" he said. "Where's Ollie?"

I nodded in the direction of Ollie's body. Jacob looked over and then dropped his head.

"Batum?" he asked.

Neither Drew nor I replied.

"He escaped from camp just a few hours after the three of you left. Killed the free man that was with me." Jacob took a seat next to me and we sat there in silence for a few minutes. Finally he spoke. "Where is Batum?"

Drew answered sharply, "He's where he belongs, Jacob. The bastard's dead."

Jacob got up and followed Drew to the precipice. I hobbled behind. There, at the bottom of the creek bed, were Batum's charred remains.

"If you look close enough, you'll see a bullet hole through his skull. I'm the one who put it there," Drew said, "and I'll take full blame."

"But he asked you to. It's not like you murdered him," I said. "If you hadn't, he would have burned to death."

Jacob looked concerned. "He was a criminal, but after that fight in camp, you might have a difficult time persuading a judge." He paused and thought for a moment. "The only choice we have is to sink him. Logging outfits will be coming through here to salvage the downed timber, so burying him isn't an option. Give me a hand, Drew."

The two of them wrapped Batum's corpse in some scrap pieces of burlap from Jacob's pack and tied some large rocks to him. After he was all bundled up, they floated him out to the middle of the lake on a couple of small timbers then sunk him. No words were said, no remorse shown. Just a piece of clay dumped in to the depths of Little Lost Lake.

"We should build a stretcher to take Ollie back to camp," I said as they stepped back on shore.

"That's just going to raise questions," Jacob said. "People are going to want to know how he died." We stood in silence, numb and emotionless. "We'd be better off burying him up here."

"He'd like that," Drew said. "We can bury him under Mr. Miller's tamarack." The fire had singed its bark, giving it a black coat around the base, but it had survived.

Drew carried Ollie around the lake to the towering tamarack as Jacob and I followed, Jacob carrying the pulaskis for digging, and me negotiating the terrain the best I could. We found Mr. Miller's brother's grave at the foot of the tamarack just as he had said. A crude cross made out of rocks was all that signified the grave.

We dug a hole in the charred ground, wrapped Ollie in a couple of Jacob's blankets, and gently lowered his body down. Save for the snap of still burning trees, we stood in silence. Drew eventually knelt down at the grave's edge.

"I wish I had some words to say, little man, but I don't. You seemed to always have enough to say for all of us. If your father were here, he'd read from the Good Book. Your mother would be crying, but still comforting the rest of us. You deserve a better burial, Oliver Hunt. A casket with flowers in a proper cemetery." Drew's voice broke and tears came. "Anyway, this is the best we can do for now, my friend. But we'll be back to visit. You can count on that."

Drew got to his feet and the three of us stared into the grave, tears rolling off our faces and dropping onto the freshly dug soil. Overhead, thunderclouds clapped, majestically announcing rain. The raindrops sizzled as they hit burning embers, starting slowly, then picking up their pace, soaking the land.

Chapter 27

(North Idaho, Fall, 1979)   J.D. and Lenny pulled into the St. Maries Memorial cemetery, the old pickup creaking as they bumped over the disheveled road.   The sod on Grandpa's grave was in place, making it more difficult to locate, even though the funeral had only been the day before. Lenny finally spotted it and they pulled up beside it. He shut off the engine.

"So that's what it was all about, J.D.?" He gave me a puzzled look. "The envelope you slipped into his coffin. It was the one from Mrs. Sorensen's class, wasn't it? Grandpa must have given it to you, and he must have promised to kill Batum. Am I right?"

"That you are, Lenny Dougherty.   Your granddad gave it to me the night of graduation. He asked me to hold on to it, but not read it."

"Why didn't he just hang on to it?   You know, put it under his mattress or something."

"After we returned from Avery, he didn't mention it, so neither did I. After a couple of years, I thought about throwing it away, but instead I put it in one of my letter boxes and forgot about it.   It wasn't until just a few days ago, when your granddad's health was fading fast that I remembered it. If I put it in his coffin things would once and for all be put to rest."

"Did you ever make it back up there to visit Ollie's grave?"

"The following summer, the day after Anna's graduation, we made our fist trip back. Ollie's ma and pa joined us, along with Phoebe, Isabel, Anna, Handy, Mr. Miller and Jacob Schilling. Handy and I made headstones out of polished stones and wrought iron for both Ollie and Mr. Miller's brother. Then, each year following, the day after the school's graduation, Drew would make the trek. I went with him the first few years, but after moving away, I couldn't manage the trip. Your granddad made his last trip this past summer."

"And no one ever knew what happened to Batum but you three?"

"We swore ourselves to secrecy. Now everyone who could be affected by it is dead, except me and your grandma."

"What about Edward and his crew. And the sheriff?"

"Edward's crew wasn't able to stop the fire at Setzer creek. Instead, it picked up momentum and overtook them. Before the fire could get to them, though, Edward holed them up in a cave. He was definitely one of the heroes of the fire. All but two of his crew survived." He shifted in his seat. "The sheriff and his crew of convicts perished."

"And the fire? Did it stop when the rains came?"

"It did, but not after killing 86 men, 57 buried here in St. Maries. There's the memorial we erected in their honor." He pointed to a large concrete pillar encircled by headstones. "There are a lot of families represented there."

"Is Ollie's name on it?"

"Yes. Even though the body was left at Little Lost Lake, they honored him with a headstone."

"What about Batum?"

"Because they couldn't find the body, they figured he'd fled into Montana or south toward Boise. Nobody was in any hurry to argue for finding him."

The two got out of the truck and walked over to the memorial. As they did, an elderly woman wound her way up through the rows of tombstones toward us. It was Lenny's Grandma.

"You're not still telling him lies are you, J.D.?" she said with a wink.

Lenny slipped his arm around her, looking at her through a different set of eyes. She looked down and saw they were standing at Ollie's headstone at the 1910 memorial.

"He's been telling me about their trip to Avery, Grandma."

She nodded.   Holding hands, Grandma, Lenny and J.D. walked over to Grandpa's grave and stood beside it.   An afternoon mist had settled in, bringing a light rain.

"Thanks, J.D." Lenny said.

"For what?"

"Bringing my grandfather alive."

"Keep those memories, Lenny Dougherty. Don't forget one detail, you hear?"

"I won't, J.D."

"Andrew and Oliver were good friends, weren't they, Jackson?" Grandma said softly.

"They sure were, Anna."

About the Author . . .

Edward Craner grew up in the small Wash farming towns of Pullman, Washtucna, and P and finished his high school and undergr work in Cheney, which is just outside of S] During these growing-up years, he and his took frequent trips to the Idaho panhandle relatives and camp on the St. Joe River. Edwa lives in San Antonio, Texas, with his wife, and two sons, Nathan and Nicholas.

Also by the Author . . .

There's Nothing Gross About Profit is a book that teaches principles and tools to competitive *view* of business owners and m This *view* enables them to convert ma opportunities in order to sustain profitability. Written in a conversational book provides real-world examples, workin and practical insight to the reader. Purcha *Nothing Gross About Profit* at:
www.booksurge.com or www.amazon.com